finding tomorrow

BAY

DENISE GROVER SWANK

NEW YORK TIMES BESTSELLING AUTHOR

A N D

CHRISTINE GAEL

finding
tomorrow

Bluebird
BAY

1

Chapter One

Home sweet home.

Celia Burrows stepped through the front door of her house with a sigh.

Part of her was happy to be back in Bluebird Bay, but she couldn't shake the unexpected sense of melancholy that had settled over her on the ride home. She'd had an amazing couple of days recharging at the Lotus Blossom Spa and Wellness Retreat with her friend, Jackie. Her skin felt great, she'd slept like a baby, and she'd had seventy-two hours to focus wholly on herself for the first time in years. But all of that *me* time hadn't recharged her like she'd hoped it would. She was already looking ahead to the yawning stretch of the week to come.

Nate always got on her about that. *"You can never live in the moment,"* he'd say.

Still, she couldn't ignore the niggling feeling that something was missing. Truth be told, the feeling had been there for years, but raising children and tending to Nate had helped drown it out. Caring for her ailing father had done the same.

She'd hoped the spa weekend would help, but if anything, that feeling seemed more insistent. *Louder.*

"Yeah, poor you, Celia," she murmured with a low chuckle under her breath as she set her suitcase in the foyer and hung her lightweight sweater on the bannister. "Stuck in this big, beautiful, dream beach house with your handsome, successful husband. Someone cue the violins."

It only caught her then that the house was extra quiet. Nate's car hadn't been in the driveway when she'd pulled up, but that didn't explain why her cocker spaniel, Tilly, hadn't charged over, tail thumping, the second she'd walked in.

"Tilly, Mommy's home," she called as she turned to scan the marble kitchen island for a note from Nate. She glanced at her watch with a frown. She'd told him what time she'd be home, and he hadn't mentioned going out. "Tilly, come on, sweet girl!" she called, cupping her hand to her mouth and calling up the stairs.

Maybe her sweet pup had missed her so much, she'd decided to hibernate in the master bedroom where Celia's scent was the strongest. That dog hadn't been without her a single day since she'd gotten her from the shelter five years before. Maybe she thought she'd been abandoned again?

Guilt pricked at her as she grabbed her suitcase and jogged lightly up the stairs. But her guilt was quickly replaced with concern as she stepped into the bedroom.

Tilly was nowhere to be found.

Dog and car, both gone. Nate would never put her in his beloved Porsche unless the dog was sick or dying...

So where were they?

She peered around the room again and a strange sensation washed over her...a sense of foreboding so strong, it made her knees go weak. The bed was made, no surprise there, as Nate had always been pretty tidy, but it looked so

picture-perfect, it could've graced the cover of *Better Homes and Gardens*.

She walked gingerly toward the king-sized bed, which seemed larger and more ominous with every step she took. Fingers trembling, she lifted the corner of the comforter, and what she found shook her to the core.

Pristine sheets with perfectly executed hospital corners.

Corners so precise, only one person could've done them, and that was Celia herself.

Blood roared in her ears, crowding out the oppressive silence. Nate hadn't slept in their bed all weekend. She'd spoken to him just yesterday morning, and he specifically told her he'd slept in and planned to spend the day working on the boat so not to worry if he didn't answer his phone. No mention of sleeping anywhere but home.

She turned to peer around the room again and something on her vanity table caught her eye. A heather gray envelope propped there, from the gorgeous, custom stationary set she'd bought Nate for Father's Day last year.

Her legs moved as if of their own accord, carrying her toward the fussy little vanity table even though her brain urged her to run in the other direction. She reached for the note gingerly, like it was a bomb, because in the deepest part of her soul, she knew that's exactly what it was.

A bomb that was going to obliterate her whole life.

She glanced down at the masculine scrawl on the front of the silky envelope that simply read, *Celia*. Then she tore it open.

Dear Celia,
It breaks my heart to do this to you this way, but I know how strong inertia is, and how easy it would be to fall back into

our normal patterns if I tried to do it in person. I love you and always will, but I'm not in love with you anymore.

The rest of the words blurred before her eyes as the note slipped from her fingertips to the gleaming, oak floor.

How could this be happening? They'd just celebrated thirty years of marriage three months before. He'd even made a toast at the party he'd insisted on throwing. In front of all their friends and family and his business associates, he'd said, *"Thirty down, thirty more to come, and I can't wait. Love you, Celia."*

But I'm not in love with you anymore.

Celia lowered herself to the vanity stool and pressed her face in her hands. This couldn't be happening. Not like this. Not now.

They finally had everything they'd ever wanted. All their hard work and sacrifice had paid off. Nate's business was booming and had become one of the premiere commercial real estate agencies in town. They'd just finished renovating their forever home, a stunning contemporary house with an unparalleled view of the ocean, now equipped with every modern convenience imaginable. The kids were grown and doing great. Max was an accountant in Portland, Maine, two and a half hours south of Bluebird Bay, and happily married to her job, for the moment. Gabe had a great fiancée, and owned a charter fishing boat that allowed him to be on the water seven days a week.

This was supposed to be their time to reconnect. Enjoy the fruits of their labor.

Together.

A sharp rap sounded at the front door and she sucked in a steadying breath.

There were only a handful of people who would stop by on a Sunday morning without calling first. Gabe was likely out on his boat, and Max typically spent the weekends with her friends. It had to be one of her younger sisters. Anna was in town between assignments, so it could be either of them.

Briefly, she considered ignoring it, but her car was in the driveway, and her sisters were nothing if not persistent.

She slipped off her kitten heels, afraid her still-wobbly legs couldn't carry her steadily, and then padded barefoot down the sleek staircase. As she passed the long mirror on the wall, she slowed and swiped at the tears she hadn't even realized were streaking down her cheeks.

No one liked to see a weeping woman—it made people uncomfortable.

The knocking grew more insistent and she quickened her pace. Maybe she was wrong. Maybe one of the kids needed help with some kind of an emergency.

Dear God, the kids.

She had been so preoccupied with her own feelings, she hadn't even considered theirs. What was she going to tell them?

Her heart gave a squeeze as memories pelted her brain like tiny, unerringly accurate bullets.

Nate holding a plump, newborn Gabe in his arms, beaming with pride. The two of them playing catch in the tiny swatch of backyard behind their starter home. Max and her daddy dressed to the nines for her kindergarten Father-Daughter dance.

Celia's chest ached so much, it felt like it might crack in half. This was bad. No doubt about it. But whoever was behind that door didn't deserve to bear the brunt of her grief.

She straightened and threw her shoulders back as she smoothed a hand through her hair.

Answer the door, plead a headache, and get whoever it is out of here as quickly as possible.

She turned the knob, pasting a polite half-smile on her face.

"Thank God! If you didn't answer, I was going to have to eat all four of these by myself, and you know I'd do it. Do you have any idea how hard it is to get a good bagel in this town?" Anna demanded as she pushed past her in a whirlwind of typical, infectious energy.

Celia tried to form a reply as she trailed behind her youngest sister, but her throat was locked up tight, frozen with unshed tears.

Keep it together, Celia, you can do this, she counselled herself silently. *You have to talk to Nate before you tell anyone. Spreading the news will only make things awkward once he comes home.*

"Tell me about the spa. Was it as glorious as I hear it is?" Anna asked as she set the white paper bag on the kitchen island and made her way toward the refrigerator. "You have cream cheese, yes?"

Celia cleared her throat and nodded. "Y-yes. On the door."

Anna set the tub of cream cheese on the marble island and then paused, butter knife in hand, hazel eyes narrowing. "You look weird. Pale. Did you eat some bad seaweed at that spa or something?"

Celia shook her head and tried to croak out a reassuring *"I'm fine."* But what came out was a wrenching, whole-body sob.

"Celia, oh my God, what's happened?" Anna asked, her face a mask of confused concern. "Is someone hurt?" Her eyes widened as she clutched at Celia's arm in fear. "Dead?"

"No, no," she managed, holding on to her sister like a lifeline. "N-Nate is leaving me."

Where were those dang violins now?

ANNA STARED AT HER SISTER, shocked into total silence.

If she was being honest, her first reaction was relief. Not because she disliked Nate—though she did—but because her mind had instantly shot to several worst-case scenarios. Gabe had gotten into a boating accident, or Max had gotten into a car wreck, or Pop had...

She pushed those thoughts away and tried to think straight, despite the fear-induced dump of adrenaline pumping through her veins.

"Okay. Okay," she mumbled, pulling her sister into a tight hug as she processed this new information.

Nate had always been a thorn in her side. He was nice to her, of course. Cee-cee wouldn't have allowed him to be anything but. Cee-cee and Anna had always been close growing up. Even now, with Anna traveling three hundred plus days a year for her job as a nature photographer, she and her oldest sister talked every week. They saw each other frequently whenever Anna returned to her home base between jobs. Nate had known that bond was unbreakable, so he'd carefully maintained the status quo. Deep down, though, Anna knew he'd never liked her.

Well, bully for him, because the feeling was mutual.

She thought back to Cee-cee, B.N.—before Nate. The girl who used to wake her and Stephanie up in the middle of

the night for a giggling skinny dip in the pool. The girl who used to host her own version of *Chopped* on their old camcorder before the show was even invented, laughingly demanding that the three of them make a meal out of canned ham, chickpeas, and peanut butter or something equally vile.

Cee-cee, B.N. had been a firecracker.

Their sister Stephanie had always thought their oldest sister might become an actress or an artist. Something creative, like Anna, because she always saw the beauty in the world.

Nate had been drawn to that wonder and light. At first, Anna had thought it was because he believed it was as beautiful as she did. It hadn't taken her long to realize that Cee-cee was just another beautiful object for him to add to his collection, like his lawn and his car and this house. He liked all of his things pristine, perfectly manicured at all times, and his wife was no exception.

Celia had been no different. She was still a gem under all the polish, but he'd done his best to keep the wildest parts of her under wraps. Anna remembered, though.

Once Nate came along, that all changed. He'd treated her like a princess, no denying that, but he'd made it clear he expected her to act the part. For a beach-loving, small-town girl who preferred a good, sticky barbecue to fine dining, wasn't that the cruelest twist of the knife? He'd done it so skillfully, changing her slowly over the years, that Anna was pretty sure Cee-cee hadn't even realized what was happening. Like a boiling frog, not that Celia, P.N.—post Nate—would appreciate the comparison.

Just watching how he treated her sister was enough to make him a fixture on her "Nope List," but she'd suffered his presence with cool politeness.

Not anymore, though. Now, she could openly hate his guts.

Her sister's trim body trembled in her arms as she wept, and Anna's hand reflexively tightened on the knife resting there. If he was nearby, she would've done a lot more than butter him with it right now, that was for sure.

Speaking of being nearby...

"Where is the bast—where is he, anyway?"

"I don't know," Celia whispered, pulling away as she swiped at her watery brown eyes. "He wasn't here when I got home. He left a note—"

"A note?" Anna demanded, hot rage coursing through her. "He left a *freaking* note? What kind of person..." She trailed off at the sight of her sister's devastated face and tried to hide her anger.

Going off on Nate wasn't going to make Cee-cee feel any better right now. And for all she knew, this was another phase in his ludicrous mid-life crisis, like the Porsche and that stupid goatee. Temporary insanity. If they got back together, anything Anna said now would become a wedge between her and her sister. So not worth it.

"You won't have to deal with him much," Cee-cee said with a sniffle. "You're leaving soon for your next assignment in Bolivia."

Anna swallowed a sigh and shook her head as she took Cee-cee's hand and squeezed. "Not going to happen. I'm going to be here for as long as you need me."

Even as she spoke the words, she felt the invisible shackles closing over her, tightening with every breath. She'd only come back because she'd heard the tension in Celia's voice the last time they'd discussed Pop's declining mental health. It was meant to be a short visit. Long enough to give Celia a much-needed break, but short enough that she

wouldn't become like her sister in the process, giving and giving to everyone else, until there was nothing left.

They'd watched their mother do it all their lives, until she was nothing but a dried-up husk of a woman. So insubstantial that even her death from breast cancer had been unremarkable. She'd just faded away, her heart growing weaker until she was gone, like a puffy, white dandelion in the breeze.

It had been so hard on all of them, although it had hit Stephanie, a real Mama's girl, the hardest. Of course, Stephanie had suffered other losses, too.

Anna wondered if Celia had actually processed their mother's death—she'd seemed so intent on healing the rest of them she'd shortchanged her own grief.

Anna cleared her throat and refocused on Celia, who was already shaking her head vehemently.

"Sis, you don't have to do that. It's fine—"

"Shut up, Cee-cee," she snapped, jerking back to glare at her sister. "It's not fine. And it won't be for a while. Just once in your life, can you put your own wants and needs first? Geez Louise, your husband of thirty years just left you, you've got Dad to deal with, and it's going to be a long, ugly summer. Let me help you. Can you do that?"

Celia wet her lips and nodded slowly as she raked a hand through her long, chestnut hair. "Yeah. Okay, I can do that."

"Perfect. First order of business, where is this *note?*" she asked, her tone pure acid.

"Upstairs. I didn't even read the whole thing, to be honest. I was so…"

"I understand. You make us some tea or something. I'm going to go up and get it, and we'll figure out where to go from there, all right?"

Celia nodded again and managed a tiny smile. "Thanks, sis."

"That's what sisters are for."

By the time she got back downstairs with the note in hand, though, her whole body was tense with unchecked fury.

"Tea ain't gonna cut it," she said as she stepped back into the kitchen, resisting the urge to shred the note into a million pieces so her sister never had to read what it said.

Dear Celia,

It breaks my heart to do this to you this way, but I know how strong inertia is and how easy it would be to fall back into our normal patterns if I tried to do it in person. I love you and always will, but I'm not in love with you anymore.

I'm sure we've both felt this growing distance between us, so this can't be much of a surprise. For what it's worth, the past thirty years with you has been my honor and I will always think on it fondly. I hope you will too…

Because this town is full of gossips, I wanted to be the one to tell you that, while I've continued to honor my vows to you, I'm ashamed to admit I've been having an emotional affair with Amanda Meadows. We plan to move our relationship forward now that you're aware.

P.S.

Since you weren't home and Amanda has a cocker spaniel of her own, I took Tilly so she wouldn't be lonely. We can talk about sharing custody of the dog once you take some time to process and get into a good, healthy place with our new normal.

Everlasting affection,
Nate

He took.

Her *dog*.

The dog he hadn't even wanted and barely gave the time of day.

Anna barreled around the kitchen, opening cabinets and slamming drawers in search of liquor. No hard stuff, but eventually she found an unopened bottle of champagne chilling in the wine cooler and a jug of orange juice in the fridge.

Morning mimosas. How utterly sophisticated. Nate would approve.

On that note, she pried the cork from the bottle, slugged five gulps straight from the opening and handed it to her sister, who watched in wide-eyed silence from her perch at the kitchen island.

"You're going to want to guzzle about half of that right about now. For medicinal purposes."

She expected Celia to argue, but to her credit, she accepted the bottle wordlessly and did as she was told.

Then, with a silent prayer, Anna laid Nate's letter on the countertop in front of her sister. She couldn't watch. Instead, she paced the kitchen floor and waited.

It didn't take long.

"Amanda Meadows...*our realtor?*" Celia gasped.

The realtor who had sold them the very house they were standing in.

The house that was supposed to be their forever home.

The bitter irony wasn't lost on Anna, but she kept her expression inscrutable as she studied Celia's devastated, tear-ravaged face, which crumpled before her very eyes.

For the next ten minutes, she just let her cry it out. Ugly, wracking sobs that had her doubled over. Sobs that the Cee-cee of three days ago would've never allowed herself to indulge in. Then, once she had quieted and caught her

breath, Anna squatted at her sister's feet and forced her chin up to lock gazes with her.

"I know you're hurting right now. I can't even imagine how difficult this is. But you need to redirect that sadness and get angry. He left you after thirty years and was too much of a chicken to do it to your face. Honey, he TOOK YOUR DOG! What kind of man does that?"

Celia sniffled and, for an instant, Anna caught a glimmer of the old, spitfire Cee-cee, B.N. as she wiped away her tears.

"He did, didn't he?"

"He sure did. Let phase two of sister-helping commence," Anna announced. "We're going to that homewrecker's house and getting your damned dog back."

*C*hapter *T*wo

Amanda Meadows? Celia still couldn't wrap her head around it. She was thin, blonde, and only a decade younger, which put Amanda in her early forties. Celia could understand if she had let herself go, but she'd always been so diligent about looking her best. Nate had made it clear he expected her to maintain the perfect image, even if he'd never outright said so. He didn't have to.

"The saying that people judge a book by its cover is true," Nate had said years ago when Celia had encouraged him to go to the grocery store wearing his painting clothes—spattered jeans and an old T-shirt. *"Clients judge their professionals by the image they present to the world, and you never know when you'll run into an existing client or a potential new one. You always want to put your best foot forward."* The look he'd given her own jean shorts and T-shirt had made it clear his lecture was meant for both of them.

The importance of maintaining appearances was so central to his life, it had slowly but surely become ingrained in Celia's psyche. She no longer owned a T-shirt or pair of jeans. When she took Tilly on their walks on the beach, she

wore a cute pair of capris and a blouse in the summer, and a cashmere sweater and slacks in the winter. No slacking for Celia Burrows.

She made sure she got to the gym four times a week and played tennis whenever the weather permitted. The second her dark hair showed a hint of silver, she was at the salon. So if Celia was at peak condition for a woman in her early fifties, why would Nate trade her in for a woman only slightly younger? It made no sense. After all they'd been through…all they'd built?

Tears burned her eyes and her sister's face became blurry. She'd spent her entire life making Nate happy and he'd just tossed her to the side like a piece of Tilly's poo…which he'd never bothered to pick up before.

"Oh, no you don't," Anna said in a stern voice. "This isn't a time for crying. It's a time for action." When Celia didn't immediately respond, she added, "Think of Tilly, Cee-cee. Think of your dog."

An unexpected fury rose up in Celia, which shot a jolt through her system. She'd spent years keeping her emotions under control, and now in a matter of less than an hour, she was experiencing two vastly different extremes. Sorrow, she was familiar with, but rage? Rage was unladylike, yet here she sat at the gleaming marble island of her ultra-modern kitchen, aching to burn or stab something.

Celia grabbed the champagne bottle from her sister's hand, then took another long swig, the bubbles tickling the back of her throat. She'd bought this champagne to celebrate the upcoming anniversary of her and Nate's first date. How ironic she was drinking it to celebrate their demise.

Setting the bottle on the counter with more force than she'd intended—she was already tipsy, God help her—she stood and straightened her back. "Let's go get Tilly."

"Do you know where this woman lives?" Anna asked, then grimaced as she glanced at the champagne. At least a third of it was gone. "We should probably take an Uber."

"No need for that," Celia said as she headed for the back entrance that led to the beach, sitting on the sleek bench to put on her walking shoes. "The homewrecker lives two blocks down the beach."

After she slipped on her shoes, she stormed out the door, leaving Anna to follow. Her sister fell in beside her, and to Celia's surprise, Anna had brought the champagne bottle.

Celia couldn't suppress the giggle that rose up inside her. A giggle! Like she was seventeen years old again, sneaking a bottle of peach-flavored vodka from her parents' liquor cabinet. She should be horrified, but instead, she snatched the bottle and took another gulp.

"I take it you hadn't suspected," Anna asked softly.

"No. But I should have known something was up," Celia conceded, now feeling like a fool. "Nate's been taking Tilly for regular walks on the beach lately. I thought he was trying to bond with her to make me happy, but deep down, I knew it was strange. He never gave her the time of day before."

And then there was the way he'd started attending more client dinners, always without her. Nate used to call her his lucky charm. She'd closed more than a few deals for him by convincing the wives, and sometimes husbands as more women took the business world by storm, of his clients that he was the guy to get the job done. But she couldn't remember the last time he'd invited her along.

He'd told her that the business world was changing—spouses attending meetings was old-fashioned. She'd believed him, but now she wondered if it were true.

She stopped in her tracks, her feet sinking into the damp sand she'd stepped in.

What if Nate was embarrassed of her?

Anna came to a halt, worry filling her eyes as she examined Celia's face. "What?"

"Am I old, Anna?" Celia asked, her voice breaking. "What if Nate's ashamed of me?"

Anger morphed Anna's face into a war mask. "If he's ashamed of you, then the man's a fool. He doesn't deserve you."

"But why? Why did he leave me?" Celia hadn't meant for it to come out as a whine, yet there it was anyway, one more slip in her perfect persona. Ladies never, *ever* whined. "What am I going to do?"

Anna grabbed both of Celia's arms and stared her deep in the eyes. "I don't know why the fool left you, but one thing I *do* know is that you *will* survive this, Celia. You're one of the strongest people I know."

Celia could see why her sister believed that. She'd worked hard to cultivate that part of her image, too. When the kids were in school, she'd headed up the PTA, and she'd chaired multiple charities over the years, always making sure that Nate's business was a featured sponsor. ("It's good for my business to look charitable," Nate had often said. "Everyone loves a community-involved business.") Volunteer work filled her schedule, even more so since the kids had left home, and she was also the primary caregiver for Pop, a task that was becoming progressively more difficult due to his early onset dementia.

The world saw Celia Elizabeth Sullivan Burrows as a competent, capable, strong woman and now her carefully controlled world was crashing down around her.

Anna gave her a little shake. "You can do this, Cee-cee, but let's take it one step at a time. First up is Tilly."

The reminder that Nate had dared to take her dog reignited her fire so hot that the imaginary flames could have burnt her eyebrows. "Who the heck does he think *he is?*" Celia demanded, pulling out of her sister's grasp. "*Stealing* my dog!"

"That's right," Anna shouted. "Stealing your dog! Let's go!" She took off stomping, and when Celia didn't immediately join her, she reached back for Celia's wrist and dragged her along.

Thinking of Tilly and that God-awful note, Celia forced her feet to work.

They passed the bottle between them again.

"What are you going to say when you see him?" Anna asked.

What *was* she going to say? The question nearly stopped Celia short, but Anna kept on marching, and Celia hurried to keep up. She wasn't going to cry, that was for certain. Nate hated her tears, and she wasn't about to give him the satisfaction of seeing that he'd broken her. That thought brought a resurgence of heat to her gut. He *hadn't* broken her. She hadn't spent years building up her image to resemble an immovable flag pole in a Nor'easter, just to fall to pieces because he'd chosen to trade her in.

Everyone had a defining moment in their lives and this would be Celia's. She'd be even stronger than before.

As soon as she got her dog back.

She was still in mission mode as she turned away from the ocean, heading up the beach toward a picture-perfect

beach cottage painted the palest of pinks, fifty feet from the high-tide mark.

"This is it?" Anna asked, her voice firm, but Celia could hear the wobble.

"Yep," Celia said, stopping at the base of the steps to the deck. She headed up before she chickened out.

"Tell her Barbie called and she wants her dream house back," Anna cracked as she started to follow her up, but Celia turned around abruptly, nearly losing her balance. She grabbed onto the railing to steady herself.

"No. You stay down here. I need to do this on my own."

Uncertainty drifted over Anna's face, and even in her alcohol-induced haze, Celia realized Anna didn't think she could do this. While the world saw Celia as strong, they *didn't* see her as a wave maker. Well, Celia Burrows might have been a smoother in the past, but she was about to crash a giant tsunami into her husband's face.

Celia's back stiffened. "If I look like I'm caving, jump in, but otherwise, let me do this." Her voice wavered. "I *need* to do this."

Anna gave a sharp nod, her eyes narrowing with determination. "Go get your dog, Celia."

Celia gave her own sharp nod then spun around to march up the rest of the steps. The champagne bottle clanged against the wooden railing, reminding her that she hadn't handed it back to her sister after her last gulp. She nearly walked back down to do it...Nate would cringe at the very thought of a lady drinking from the bottle, but her tipsiness was increasing by the second, and suddenly, she didn't give a rat's crack.

Ladies didn't make scenes, either, and Celia was about to make a big, stinky one.

The middle of Amanda's house featured a row of three French doors that opened to a stellar view of the ocean. Celia walked to the middle set of doors and knocked loudly.

Tilly came running over, scratching on the glass in a frantic effort to get to her owner. It took everything in Celia to ignore Tilly and focus on the shocked expression of the man walking through the living room toward her. He was wearing Bermuda shorts, for heaven's sake!—and shirtless to boot. Amanda trailed behind, wearing a short, blue silk nightdress with spaghetti straps.

Nate froze when he realized who was banging on the door, then hurried closer, scooping up Tilly and cradling her before he opened the door. The image of her precious pup in his arms looked *so wrong*, it only made her angrier.

Why was he pretending to love her dog?

Why did he pretend to love me?

"Celia?" Nate said, looking her up and down and seeming even more confused.

Celia glanced down, not surprised by his bewilderment. She was wearing her pale pink Clarks shoes with her tan linen pants and she was sure her hair was as wrecked as her mascara. Her back stiffened as her gaze jerked up to his.

"You can walk out of my life like the coward you are, Nathan Burrows, but how *dare you* think you could take my dog?"

His mouth dropped open like a fish, his eyes bulging in shock. No wonder. Celia was certain she'd never spoken to him in such a direct way in their entire relationship.

"*Your* dog?" Amanda demanded from behind him, her cocker spaniel trying to get past her onto the deck. "Matilda is *Nathan's* dog."

Celia took a step backward as disbelief slammed into her. She struggled to keep her balance. "Who's Matilda?" she asked, turning her attention to the blonde. "Is that what he told you Tilly's name is?"

Amanda gave Celia a pitying look. "While you call her Tilly, Nathan says he prefers to use her given name."

Celia's brow wrinkled as she put it together, then she burst out laughing.

Nate looked like he wanted to bury himself under a giant sand castle.

"What's so funny?" Amanda asked, then turned to Nate. "Why is she laughing like that?"

Nate finally seemed to come to his senses, pointing to the bottle in Celia's hand. "She's *drunk*." Disgust washed over his face. "Go home, Celia. I'm not coming back with you, and you're making a fool of yourself."

"Making a fool of *myself*?" Celia demanded with a short laugh. "You're the one lying to your *mistress*." She spat it out like it was a dirty word.

"It wasn't like that," Nate said, his tone softening. Tilly began to struggle in his arms, trying to get free. "We didn't sleep together."

"Until you moved *in here*, at least," Celia sneered. If he had been telling the truth about their lack of a physical relationship, their current attire indicated that ship had officially sailed. "Were you throwing your suitcases in the car as soon as Jackie picked me up on Friday afternoon?"

His cheeks went ruddy. She'd been fishing, but it was obvious that she'd guessed right. "Celia, I know this is hard for you to understand—"

"That's right," Celia said, poking him in the chest over Tilly's back. "It *is* hard for me to understand why you slunk away like a little weasel after thirty years of marriage. You couldn't be bothered to tell me to my face, and then had the nerve to steal *my*"—she shot a glare to Amanda then back to Nate—"dog!"

Tilly finally squirmed free and leapt from Nate's arms onto the deck, trotting around Celia and sitting behind her feet. The show of solidarity from her four-legged friend bolstered Celia's courage.

"Her name is *Tilly*, and it has been since *I* adopted her five years ago after Max moved out. The dog you never wanted and barely tolerated." She shot a glare to her husband. "I can't believe you had the audacity to tell her that Tilly was *yours*!"

"Well, of course she is," Amanda said as though Celia's argument was preposterous. "Nate walks her on the beach every night because you can't be bothered to do it. My spaniel Heather and I have walked with him every night for the past three months."

Ah, there it was—her suspicion had been spot on, although she took no pleasure from it. This explained her husband's sudden enthusiasm to take over Tilly's nightly walks at a precise time—7:40. He'd told her it was for health reasons, and when she'd offered to go with him, he'd insisted she take a bath or watch her favorite TV show instead, finally telling her it was his alone time to unwind and reflect on the day. Turned out he'd been reflecting on Amanda Meadows instead.

"So you lied to her, too?" Celia said, becoming firmer in her resolve. "You lied to us both."

Nate's face paled. "Uh…"

"The details aren't important to me," Amanda said, draping herself against Nate's side, her bright red fingernails resting against Nate's bare arm.

Red nails? Nate hated polish. He said it looked trashy.

Amanda gave Celia another pitying look. "He was miserable with you, but he's happy with me. We love each other."

Celia nodded as she took this all in, her emotions shifting in her head like a game of Tetris. Her anger had settled down, and her need for revenge now reared its ugly head.

"Just so I'm clear," Celia said, narrowing her gaze on her husband. "You want to leave me and move in with Amanda. This is permanent?"

Nate's face flushed. "Celia..."

"It's a yes-or-no question, Nate," she said, cutting him off.

He looked surprised by her direct tone. He was used to her acquiescence. "Yes," he said as though speaking to a child. "I know you'd rather we keep going the way we were, but—"

She put her thumb over the top of the champagne bottle and began to shake. "The explanation isn't necessary," she said, "I just wanted to make sure I had this perfectly clear." She gave them both a sugary smile. "Congratulations to you both. Here's a toast to your happiness." Releasing her thumb, she let the rest of the champagne spray onto the happy couple, although the fizz wasn't as satisfying as Celia had hoped, since the bottle had been open and was nearly two-thirds gone. She flung the rest of the contents on him with several shakes.

Amanda shrieked in high-pitched wails. "My silk nightgown. You've ruined it!"

Celia dropped the bottle onto the deck with a satisfying thud. "Send me a bill. Or better yet, let Nate's divorce lawyer handle it, because I'll be filing for divorce first thing tomorrow morning." She swallowed hard and forced the question she'd been dreading to ask past her lips. "Do the kids know?"

He shifted from foot to foot, refusing to meet her gaze. "No, not yet."

"Given your track record of delivering this news in a healthy fashion, I'm going to suggest I be the one to tell them. You know, so they don't spend the rest of their lives in counseling."

"What are you going to tell them?" he asked, a sick expression on his face.

"I guess you'll have to wait and see, won't you?" Celia squatted to pick up Tilly, burying her face in the pup's fur. She breathed deeply and released a cough. Her dog smelled like cheap perfume and cigarette smoke. Poor Tilly would be getting a bath as soon as she got her home. The dog squirmed loose and took off down the steps, seemingly as eager to get away from this place as Celia was.

With that, Celia spun around to follow, thankful she didn't fall on her face. That would definitely have ruined the effect of her show-stopping flounce.

Tromping down the steps, Celia beamed at the stunned expression on her sister's face. Anna likely didn't think Celia had it in her. Truth be told, Celia hadn't known she had, either. Not really. She was elated to find a piece of the girl she'd been before Nate's expectations—and her own—had crushed it out of her.

"Who names a dog Heather?" Anna asked, cackling as she struggled to keep up with Celia's long, determined strides.

Tilly ran a bit ahead of them as though trying to put as much distance between herself and Nate as possible.

"Right?" Celia said with a grimace.

"And I'm staying with you tonight, by the way," Anna added.

"I'm fine," Celia said, but the high of her act of rebellion was already beginning to fade, and her doubts and insecurities had begun to slip in. She was fifty-two years old and hadn't worked since Gabe was born twenty-eight years ago. She'd never lived alone. *Ever.* How would she handle a big empty house? She'd barely handled the quiet when she'd walked in the door less than two hours before.

Goodness, had it only been two hours since her life imploded?

"I know. You're always fine, but I'm still staying," Anna said.

The silence stretched between them as reality began to sink in through the rage and champagne-induced haze.

"You're strong," Anna said. "You'll survive this, Cee-cee. I promise."

Would she?

She'd spent the past thirty years centering her entire world on her husband and kids, and now she was alone without a purpose. Without a man. Without a job. Without an identity.

She was terrified.

Chapter Three

You're going to be okay, Shelley," Stephanie murmured as she finished cleaning the final wound on the massive turtle's front leg.

The assurance was as much for herself as it was for the turtle. Truth was, despite her nearly three decades in veterinary medicine, she had no clue if the animal would make it. He had certainly looked like a goner an hour ago.

Beckett Wright, from Beckett's Towing, had brought "Shelley" into her practice on the back of his flatbed after spotting him on the side of the road, bloody and motionless. The turtle's shell had a jagged crack that spanned almost the whole length of the poor creature, and his flesh had so many lacerations, she'd stopped counting. Probably had been clipped by an eighteen-wheeler, because if it were something smaller, she was pretty sure Beckett would've wound up towing the vehicle *and* the turtle. Shelley was the size of a small kitchen table and would've done some serious damage to almost anything that hit him.

To her surprise, despite his wounds, when she and Beckett had hoisted the barely breathing animal off the truck and onto the gurney, he'd put up a feeble protest. Just enough to let her know that he wasn't ready to give up the ghost yet. And if Shelley was willing to fight, so was she.

She patted the sedated turtle's leathery head and stood back to eye her handiwork. It would have to do for now, until Mick brought in the items she'd requested.

She spared a glance at the clock. Another fifteen minutes before he was due. Just long enough to wash up and get a cup of coffee.

Stephanie straightened and pressed a hand to her stiff lower back. It wasn't even noon yet, but it had already been a long day. Between paperwork and two emergency calls before Shelley's abrupt arrival, she'd put in six hours so far and had another three ahead of her just to get the billing done.

When she got home, she'd spend some quality time with what Cee-cee referred to as her "menagerie" before she zoned out in front of the TV, exhausted.

A perfect Sunday.

She tried to do that every day, really. If she packed her days full of activity from sun up to sun down, she'd only have a few hours to dwell on all she'd lost.

Her heart gave a squeeze as an image of Paul's face skated through her mind.

Had it been two years already? Some days, the wound felt like it was healing, the sharp edge of grief growing just a little less agonizing. Then she would open the bedroom closet and see his favorite cable-knit sweater hanging there and it would tear open again.

Lather, rinse, repeat.

She swallowed past the knot in her throat and tugged off her latex gloves, tossing them into the trash can before washing her hands. As she made her way out of the office and into the galley kitchenette, the phone in her whitecoat pocket chirped.

She tugged it out and glanced down.

A text from Sarah.

Just checked the weather and it's a gorgeous day there, Ma. Get out and enjoy the sunshine a little. Love you.

Her youngest daughter was a peach. The kind of kid that moms dreamed about. Valedictorian, spent almost as much time volunteering as she did doing school work, later going on to graduate magna cum laude after a full ride to law school. She was doing an internship in D.C. under the newest Supreme Court Justice.

And, as busy as she was, she never forgot to check in on her mom.

Stephanie whipped off a quick reply, promising she would take the dogs for a long walk later and sending her love back.

Of her three kids, Sarah had taken Paul's death the hardest, and Stephanie had to wonder if it was her own deep sadness some days that reminded her to touch base with her mother.

Stephanie pocketed her phone and busied herself making a pot of coffee. She was just adding creamer when the side door swung open.

"Hey, you," she said, swiping an errant curl from her face.

Mick Rafferty stepped into the room with a crooked grin on his handsome face, a can of polyurethane in one hand, tool box in the other.

"Hey, Steph. How'd it go?" One black brow rose in question and she knew what he was asking.

"The stubborn old thing is still hanging in there," she said, shaking her head in wonder. "He really wants to live."

Which would make it that much harder if she failed. She'd never liked to see animals die, but ever since Paul, each loss seemed to cut a little deeper.

"That's half the battle," he said with a satisfied nod. "Ready?"

She gestured to the pot. "Coffee?"

"Four cups already. Any more and I'll buzz right out of my skin."

"Let's get to it then."

She picked up her own cup and led him into the O.R. Shelley lay on the table, still in a medicated sleep.

Mick let out a low whistle. "He's a big one, huh?"

"Yep. Lived a long life. Let's see if we can't make it longer."

It wasn't often that she asked a master carpenter for help at her vet practice, but Shelley's case required a little creativity. Stephanie had known Mick all her life—he'd been friendly with Cee-cee in high school, so she and Anna had gotten to know him by association. Over the years, they'd seen each other at various community functions or occasionally shared a meal when they ran into one another at Mo's Diner. He'd been her first call upon seeing the damage to Shelley, and despite his busy schedule, he hadn't hesitated to volunteer his time.

"You really think this is going to work?" he asked now, scratching at his five o'clock shadow dubiously.

"Won't know until we try."

And, for the next two hours, they tried.

Under her guidance, Mick used a tiny drill to pierce a row of holes in the turtle's shell on both sides of the crack. Then, using Mick's muscle and her skill with a needle, they threaded stiff wire through the holes, sewing the crack shut as tightly as possible.

Once they finished, Mick applied a thick line of waterproof glue to the seam.

"Good job, team. It's this next part I'm not so sure of," Mick said as he shook the can of viscous liquid.

An idea struck her and she jogged lightly out to her desk to snag a business card.

When she returned, Mick was already starting the process, brushing shellac over the animal's shell in long, even strokes.

"I'm going to put my business card underneath it so that if he gets hurt again, the person who finds him will know to bring him to me."

The plan was to release Shelley to the wild if Stephanie's crazy idea actually worked, but it would take months, maybe more, before that could happen. They would need to let all his wounds heal and see how the Franken-surgery held up in motion and under water.

Mick took the card and laid it onto a bare spot before slathering it with epoxy.

"It's going to take time to dry fully so let's give it a day before we add another," he said as he continued. "We'll need six or so coats, but he should be able to get wet and refreshed in between. I'll grab a kiddie pool from the store and drop it off later today."

"Thanks so much for everything, Mick. And now that I know how to apply that stuff, don't feel like you have to come back every time," she said hurriedly.

She didn't mind giving up hours of her time to help animals without hope of compensation, but she certainly didn't expect it of anyone else.

She should've known better because Mick shook his head briskly. "Nope. I'll be here to do it. I want to see how everything goes."

Not about to argue, she shot him a grateful smile.

He was just finishing up when her phone chimed again. This time, though, it was the urgent message tone she'd set up for clients who had emergency needs.

When she glanced down and saw it was from Anna, her guts churned.

She thumbed her finger over the screen and opened the text.

Call me. Right now.

Please, God, not Pop. Not yet. They'd lost their mother only three years ago.

Guilt rushed in as she tried to recall the last time she'd gone to see him. Weeks. He lived less than three miles away, and it had been weeks.

"Mick, I've got to take this. Be right back."

She dialed Anna, her heart beating a hundred miles an hour.

"Oh, thank God! I was sure you'd be doing surgery on a hedgehog or something," Anna said in an urgent whisper. "Everyone is fine physically, but you need to get to Cee-cee's. Like, now."

Her youngest sister had a flair for the dramatic, but despite the reassurance, something in Anna's tone only half calmed Stephanie's nerves.

"What's going on?"

"I don't have time to get into the whole story, she's in the bathroom and will be back in a sec, but I'll nutshell it for you. Nate left, took the dog with him, and is shacked up with Amanda Meadows."

The room seemed to spin and Stephanie pinched her eyes shut with a groan.

"Holy cow…"

This was a bombshell. Stephanie's relationship with Nate over the past thirty-plus years had been cordial and, if asked, he likely would have described them as friends.

He would've been mistaken. Stephanie loved her sister, her sister loved Nate, ergo... But that didn't mean she wouldn't help Cee-cee bury the body and hide the evidence if she had to.

Family was family, and that was that.

Even so, it came as a shock. Nate and Cee-cee had their problems, like most couples did, but why would he leave now, after thirty years? It made no sense. Especially after Nate had made that cheesy speech at their extravagant thirtieth wedding anniversary party a few months ago.

"Poor Cee-cee." Divorce wasn't like a death, but it was still a huge blow that had undoubtedly left her sister reeling. "Be there in twenty minutes," she said, ready to hang up the phone and get on with it.

"Bring supplies," Anna said grimly.

"Roger that."

Stephanie disconnected and pocketed her phone, already making a list in her head.

When they were younger, "supplies" had been code for comfort food. They were close in age and had gone through teen drama all around the same time. Whenever a boy hurt their feelings or one of them had some silly argument with a close friend, the three of them would sit around and watch Doctor Zhivago or some other sad movie and console themselves with ice cream and Twizzlers.

If any event called for mocha toffee crunch, it was this one.

She made her way back into the O.R. to find Mick packing up his toolbox.

"I'm so sorry, I have to run. An urgent family matter," she said, cheeks heating as she tried not to make eye contact with the always perceptive Mick.

This whole thing with Nate had just happened, and while the whole town would know soon enough, it wasn't her story to tell. After all he'd done for her today, though, she'd feel like a heel if she had to lie to him.

She needn't have worried, though. Mick took it in stride, asking simply, "Is anyone hurt?"

Someone was definitely hurt, but she shook her head, knowing what he meant. "Everyone is fine."

"Let me know if you need anything," he said with a clipped nod. "I'm done here so I can follow you out."

On her way to the store, she made a quick call to her neighbor and friend, Bev, and asked her to take the dogs for a walk. Then, twenty minutes later, almost to the second, she pulled up to her sister's house.

As she put her SUV in park, she stared at it with a critical eye. From an architectural perspective, it was kind of amazing. All sharp points and glass. A study in geometry with a killer view. But somehow, whenever she looked at it, it made her feel sad. There was no life there. No soul. She often marveled that her sister had helped design it. A visual representation of Nate's influence on her.

Not your home, not your decision, she reminded herself firmly. She was here for support, not judgement.

She grabbed her purse and scooped up the brimming grocery bag before stepping out of the car. Sarah was right. It was a gorgeous day in Bluebird Bay. She tipped her head back and took a second to enjoy the sensation of the sun on her face. It was all the time she could spare. Her sister needed her, and it was time to dive into the fray.

When she stepped into the house through the side kitchen door, she could sense the mood already. A cork sat on the countertop next to a little pool of spilled champagne, next to an unopened jug of orange juice and a wad of crumpled up tissues. Her sister was an immaculate housekeeper, so even this little mess was out of the ordinary.

"I'm here," she called as she set her purse down and began unloading and putting away the supplies.

She'd grabbed a pint of mocha toffee crunch and, on second thought, had gone back to grab two more. She'd also picked up clam chowder, some crusty bread, and an expensive box of dark chocolates, just in case they needed backup.

"We're in here," Anna called back.

Stephanie grabbed two pints of the ice cream and three spoons, closing the drawer with her hip before padding toward the sound of her sister's voice.

"Hi, sweetie," she said softly as she stepped into the living room to find Anna sprawled on a cream-colored chair and Cee-cee curled up on the couch, wrapped in a peach cashmere throw, Tilly snuggled by her side.

"Hey," Cee-cee murmured, shooting her a watery smile. "Bet this isn't what you planned to do with your Sunday, huh?" Her smile cracked and tears streamed down her lovely face, sending a stab of pain straight to Stephanie's heart.

"Aw, babe," she said as she set the supplies on the table and pulled her sister into a tight hug. "I know. I know. I'm so sorry." She stroked Cee-cee's silky hair for a while until her sister finally sniffled and pulled away.

"How about some ice cream?" Anna asked, popping off her chair and snagging a spoon and a pint. "It's guaranteed to make you feel at least ten percent better."

"I really shouldn't," Cee-cee said as she gazed at it longingly.

"Would you give it a rest?" Anna shot back, digging her spoon into the creamy mixture. "You've been eating that froyo crap for years because your perfectionist husband wanted to keep you whip-thin. One pint of the good stuff isn't going to hurt you. Live a little, sis." With that, Anna plugged a massive mound into her mouth and moaned. "So good."

Cee-cee's lips twitched and she shrugged as she leaned in and picked up the second pint. "You're totally right," she said, grabbing the other two spoons and handing one to Stephanie.

The three of them ate in companionable silence with HGTV blaring in the background for a while. Cee-cee would tell her the whole story when she was ready. Until then, she'd just be here in silent support.

Her sisters had done that for her after Paul's boating accident. She could remember it like it was yesterday. The hope. The fear. The devastation.

At first, she'd been flocked by people—helping her with the funeral, bringing her food, sending her flowers, calling her. But after the service ended and the flowers dried up and the Tupperware was all returned, it was just her, left behind in the house where they'd shared their lives. That had been the worst of it.

She glanced around and shook her head. Boy, would this massive beast of a house feel lonely for just one person.

"I've got to call the kids," Cee-cee finally said, setting down her spoon with a sigh.

"Why don't you invite them over for dinner?" Stephanie countered. "Give yourself a few hours to shower and get it together. Anna and I can fix a meal."

Cee-cee nodded and stood, seeming to appreciate the directives. Sometimes it was easier not to have to think at times like these.

"Don't let Anna cook any chicken," Cee-cee said, a hint of her old self peeking through for just long enough to give Stephanie hope that she would get through this with less scars than she expected.

"It was one time," Anna crowed, rolling to her feet in faux indignation. "And it wasn't raw, it was just...rare."

The three of them chuckled and she and Anna watched as Cee-cee trudged out of the room, still wrapped in her blanket, Tilly trailing after her.

"It's going to be a heck of a few weeks," Stephanie said with a sad smile.

"Yup. Buckle up, buttercup. We've got our work cut out for us."

Chapter Four

Celia hadn't been this nervous since her first date with Nate, which, she decided, seemed to bookend their relationship nicely.

How was she going to break it to the kids? The hardest part might be getting them to the house for dinner on such short notice. Her daughter Maxine was an accountant for a high profile national firm and was always working, trying to pay her dues so she could climb the next rung of the corporate ladder. Her son Gabe was the captain of a commercial fishing boat and took clients out for a day of deep sea fishing. Since it was Sunday, he was likely out on the water, and just as likely out of cell phone range. Thankfully, she had a plan to motivate them to come.

She'd gone to the kitchen to retrieve her phone, and Anna and Stephanie had followed her, as though they were afraid she might bolt. Without discussing it, they'd all taken seats around the granite countertop. Her sisters watched her carefully as she called Max, Tilly laying on the dog bed tucked into the corner. The little dog hadn't strayed more than a few feet from Celia since she'd come home.

"Mom," her daughter said cheerfully, but Celia could hear a bit of hesitation in her voice. "I was about to call you."

Could her daughter feel Celia's nervousness already? She always had been a sensitive child growing up. "Oh? Is everything okay?"

"Does something have to be wrong for me to call you?"

Celia's stomach tightened. "You're more a texter than a caller, only calling when something's important or serious."

"Oh." Her daughter paused for a moment. "Wow. You're so right, Mom." Her voice trailed off as though this were a major revelation.

Max's admission caught Celia off guard. What was going on today? "Okay…well…I know this is short notice, but I need you to come to dinner tonight. Seven o'clock." Which would give Gabe time to shower after his day at sea. "I'm making your favorite tuna melts."

Anna stuck her finger into her mouth and made a gagging face, while Stephanie smacked her arm and shot her a glare. Celia turned to the side to ignore them. It had been Max's favorite dinner growing up, despite Nate's dislike of it, and it was only now, in hindsight, that she wished she'd made it more often.

"Tuna melt?" Max said, her tone brightening. "I'll be there."

Celia rested her elbow on the island, cradling her chin with her hand and closing her eyes in relief. One down. One to go. "I know it's a long drive from Portland, so feel free to spend the night in the guest room and head back in the morning."

"It's like you read my mind, Mom."

Something in her daughter's voice still sounded off. That, combined with her willingness to come over at the drop of a hat, had Celia worried, but her brain was fried and she lacked the reasoning skills to untangle it all at the moment. "Good," she said. "I'll see you tonight."

"Mom, wait," Max called out before Celia could hang up.

"Yes?"

"I love you. I realize I haven't told you that much lately, either."

Tears burned Celia's eyes. "I love you, too, honey." Then she hung up and stared at her sisters. "She's coming." But she was still stuck on Max's sudden sentimentality. Had she picked up on something in Celia's voice? Or was another storm brewing in Max's world?

Please, God, not today.

"Why on earth did you tell her you were making tuna melts?" Anna asked in disgust.

"It's her favorite," Celia said absently, looking up Gabe's number, then decided to call his fiancée, Sasha, first. She was more likely to answer on a Sunday afternoon, and besides, she tended to be the one to set their social calendar.

Sasha answered but only right before the call went to voicemail. "Hello," she said, her tone more hesitant than usual.

"Sasha, honey," Celia said, telling herself to keep it together. "Do you and Gabe have plans tonight?"

"Uh…"

"I realize it's short notice, but I was wondering if you guys could make it to dinner at seven tonight. It's important."

Celia frowned after Sasha's unusually long pause. This was so unlike Sasha. She was cheerful and outgoing, the perfect counterpart to her workaholic, driven son. Why was she being so withdrawn? "Sasha, are you feeling okay?"

"Yes," she answered. "I'm fine. And don't worry. I'll tell Gabe how important it is. He'll make it in time."

"Thank you," Celia said, sinking onto her stool with relief. "Tell him I'm making his favorite," she added as an afterthought. "Spaghetti Bolognese."

"Okay," Sasha said softly and hung up.

"They're both coming, thank goodness, although there must be a full moon or something. Both Max and Sasha weren't quite themselves." Celia glanced over at her sisters, narrowing her eyes at Anna's open mouth. "What?"

"We're making two dinners?"

Celia was slightly confused for a moment then waved her hand. "I needed to get them both here, so I promised to make their favorite meals."

"But it sounded like she'd already agreed before you promised," Anna protested.

"Oh for heaven's sake, Anna," Stephanie grumped. "Let it go. I made my kids their favorite meals for months after Paul died to get them to come over."

"But on the *same night?*" Anna asked, but then quickly shut her mouth when confronted with Stephanie's glare.

"I know you said you'd cook," Celia said, feeling rudderless now that her task was done. "But I can do it. I need something to do." Maybe it would help fill the hollow feeling in her chest.

"We'll all cook together," Stephanie said with a huge smile that was obviously forced. "It will be fun. We'll put Anna in charge of the Bolognese sauce. Hopefully, she won't screw that up."

"Hey!" Anna protested.

Celia smiled, then hopped off her stool and walked around the island and pulled her sisters into a group hug. They both hugged her back, none of them saying a word. It wasn't necessary. They'd all been there for Stephanie after Paul had died, and now they were here for her.

"Go shower," Anna finally said, pulling free and wrinkling her nose. "You smell like that Love Baby Soft cologne Stephanie used to wear back in high school."

Amanda's cheap perfume that had embedded into Tilly's coat.

Tears sprang into Celia's eyes at the reminder, but then she steeled her back. She was done crying over that woman. Still, while she knew her husband was ultimately to blame, she didn't want some other woman's perfume all over her dog—or herself.

"Come on, Tilly," Celia said, sweeping out of the room. "We're both getting a shower."

The rest of the afternoon was filled with a little wine and even some laughter as Celia's sisters rallied to make her forget that her life had turned on its head, but it all came back the moment the doorbell chimed.

"Who on earth could that be?" Anna asked.

Celia looked at the clock on the microwave—6:57—and set down her wine glass. "It's probably one of the kids."

"Your children ring the doorbell?" Anna asked in horror.

Even Stephanie looked perplexed.

"W-well…" Celia stuttered. "Only after we moved into the new house." The house her children had grown up in had been their home. They'd had their own keys, which they'd used to visit whenever they pleased. But Nate had objected to continuing the arrangement at the new house, insisting the kids would set off the alarm system if they visited without calling first. Since the front door was usually locked and the house was so big, they'd begun to ring the doorbell. In hindsight, she had to wonder if the real reason he'd put up a fuss was because he hadn't wanted them to walk in without warning when she wasn't home.

Not for the first time, it crossed her mind that Nate might have been unfaithful with someone other than Amanda over the past two years. He and Celia certainly hadn't been sleeping together much…

"Never mind all that," Stephanie said. "Someone's standing outside waiting. Do you want me to get it?"

"No," Celia said, smoothing imaginary wrinkles out of her pants as she stood. "I'll do it."

She carefully made her way to the front door, realizing she'd had a little too much wine. The floor felt a tiny bit shaky under her kitten heels. When she opened the front door, Max was standing on the front step in yoga pants and a T-shirt, her hair pulled back in a messy bun. While her unkempt appearance was out of the norm, it was the two large suitcases on either side of her daughter and the overnight bag slung over her shoulder that took Celia by surprise.

"Do you really need that much stuff for one night, Maxi?" Celia blurted out, unconsciously using the nickname she'd given Max when she was a child. She hadn't called her daughter Maxi in years.

Max grimaced. "Well, about that…"

"Max!" Anna called out in greeting as she pushed her way past Celia. She grabbed one of Max's suitcases and heaved it into the house.

"Let me help," Stephanie said, rushing out to grab the other one.

Max watched her aunts in shock. "Aunt Anna," Max said, glancing from one to the other. "Aunt Stephanie. What are you both doing here? I mean, I'm always happy to see you, but Mom didn't mention…"

Celia's sisters both cast her a look, then Anna took Max's arm and led her to the kitchen. "Let's get you a drink before dinner." She cast a glance back at the suitcases, gave Celia a wide-eyed expression. "Obviously driving home isn't a concern."

"I'm fine," Max said, her nervous eyes on Celia. "I don't need a drink."

"Oh, I think tonight calls for alcohol," Anna said with a scoff. "I'll fetch you a glass of wine. White or red?"

"White," Max said, then flashed her mother a smile and wandered to the large windows overlooking the ocean. "Dad was right. The view really is stunning at dusk." Max glanced around the room, her gaze stopping at the wet bar. "Where is Dad, anyway?"

"Uh…" Celia said, suddenly unsure about everything. How was she going to tell the kids? She'd spent the entire afternoon preparing for the meal and had given little thought about what to say—and when to say it—once the kids actually arrived. It wasn't like there was a good painless way to do it, and the thought of the hurt she was about to cause them had her blinking back the hot sting of tears.

Stephanie wrapped her arm around Celia's back and gave her a reassuring squeeze. "Gabe and Sasha should be here soon," she said. "How have you been, Max? I haven't seen you since the anniversary party a few months ago." She must have realized her mistake the moment the word anniversary left her mouth because her hand tightened on Celia's arm.

A few months ago, Celia had thought her life was very nearly perfect. How could she have been so blind?

Then she met Max's gaze and the confusion on her daughter's face reminded her that it wasn't the time for self-reflection. She needed to ease her children into the news. That was the most important thing now.

But first she needed more wine. Normally, she was a one-glass social drinker. Today, though? Today, she was going to do whatever she had to in order to get through this in one piece. If that meant glass number three after a champagne drink-n-spray brunch?

So be it.

"I'll go check on Anna and dinner." Or wine. Hadn't she said she'd bring some for Max?

But she didn't get more than a step or two in before the doorbell chimed again.

Gabe and Sasha.

She turned toward the door, nearly falling from the sudden shift in equilibrium. She righted herself, only to stumble again when her heel caught the edge of a rug.

"Mom?" Max called out in alarm.

"I'm fine," Celia called over her shoulder with a wave of her hand. Then her other heel caught. Letting out a very unladylike curse, Celia kicked off her shoes, one after the other, flinging them across the room, then padded to the front door without a single mishap. That was better.

But when she opened the door, it was only a glum-faced Gabe who stood on the step, wearing a very wrinkled blue and white seer-sucker shirt and khaki pants. He cast a glance down at her bare feet, then back up to her face, shock evident in his eyes. "Where are your shoes?"

"Where's Sasha?" she countered, the alcohol and her earlier encounter with Nate giving her a confrontational edge she didn't normally possess. Nate would've called her out for going barefoot "like a hippie" with company present, too, and the last thing she needed right now was another reminder of him.

Gabe blinked in surprise at her retort, then glanced over her shoulder. "Is that Aunt Stephanie?"

"And Aunt Anna, too," Anna called out, emerging from the kitchen with Max's wine. "Let the poor boy in, Celia, dear. Dinner's ready."

Celia moved out of the entrance so Gabe could walk past her. Why was Gabe's shirt hopelessly wrinkled? More importantly, where was his fiancée?

"Why don't we go ahead and eat?" Stephanie said with a tight edge in her voice.

Celia would normally be horrified to skip pre-dinner drinks and conversation, but in this instance, it seemed the best course of action. They wouldn't skimp on wine with dinner, anyway.

Stephanie and Anna hurried in the kitchen to bring out the food, while Celia motioned for the children to head to the dining room table, which had already been set.

Celia took Nate's usual place at the head of the table. Gabe gave his sister a questioning look, which she answered with a shrug before they both sat down, flanking either side of their mother.

Anna and Stephanie emerged from the kitchen—Anna making a retching face as she carried out the tuna melt sandwiches. "I'll run and get the salad and bread," Stephanie said, setting down a large bowl of Spaghetti Bolognese.

"And I'll get more wine," Anna said as though it was the most important ingredient to the meal. Maybe she was right in this instance.

"Where's Dad?" Gabe asked. "Why are you sitting in his chair?"

"It's not *his* chair, Gabe," Max countered, leaning forward with a fire in her eyes. "Mom can sit there if she wants to."

"Well, of course she can sit there," Gabe countered in a huff. "But that still doesn't explain where Dad is, now does it?"

Celia watched her children in frustration. They'd been born fifteen months apart and had spent the better part of their childhood at each other's throats, much to Celia's dismay. Once Gabe had gone off to college, they'd outgrown it, but here they were now, resorting to old behavior. She just didn't have it in her to deal with their bickering right now.

"Where's Sasha?" Max quipped as Stephanie arrived with the salad and bread. "She get tired of you already?"

Gabe's face paled. He swallowed then glanced at Celia. Shifting his gaze back to his sister, he said, "As a matter of fact, yes."

"What?" Max asked in shock, pushing her chair back as horror washed over her face. "Gabe! I was teasing!"

"Well…" he said, glancing down at his empty plate. "I'm not."

Celia stared at her son in a state of shock. This would definitely explain Sasha's odd behavior during their phone call earlier. "Gabe," she said, her heart breaking for her visibly distraught son. "When did this happen?"

"Last week," he said, now fiddling with his fork. "And I don't want to talk about it."

"But I saw you both two weeks ago," Celia said, trying to fathom it. "Everything seemed fine." But she instantly regretted the sentiment. Wasn't that also true of her relationship with Nate? She placed a hand on his arm. "Honey, I'm so sorry."

He shrugged as he sniffed, still not looking at anyone. "Yeah…well, it's not like everyone has a perfect relationship like you and Dad."

Anna had been taking a sip of her water and began to choke.

Everyone turned to her in alarm, but Stephanie shot her a dirty look. Gesturing to the bowl of spaghetti, she said, "How about we eat?" She scooped up a heaping spoonful of noodles and sauce, then dumped it on Gabe's plate.

Max reached for a grilled sandwich, with a look of discomfort on her face.

"Is everything okay with you, Max?" Celia asked. Her daughter obviously hadn't been herself on the phone earlier, and then she'd shown up with two very full suitcases.

Celia said a silent prayer that her mother's intuition was off for once. This camel's back was already bowing. She wasn't sure how much more she could take…

"Now doesn't seem like a good time to bring it up," Max said with a grimace.

What was that old saying about bad things happening in threes?

Celia tried to quell a fresh wave of panic and gave her daughter a reassuring nod. "It's okay, Maxi. Tell me."

Max shot her brother a glance—he had picked up his fork and was twirling up some noodles—then turned back to her mother.

"Mom…I quit my job."

Chapter Five

Celia blinked, certain she'd heard wrong. "What?"

"I quit my job," Max said with more determination. It was as if admitting it had opened a floodgate, and she blurted the rest out in one rushed breath. "I've been working at Franklin and Deets since I graduated from college and I was so certain it was what I wanted, but here I am, six years later and my job is my *entire life*, Mom. There's no time for anything—or *anyone*—else. Do you know how long it's been since my last date?" When no one answered, she said, "Two years. *Two years!* How pathetic is that?"

"You saved yourself misery," Gabe muttered, still twirling noodles, though he'd yet to take a bite.

"Sorry. I didn't mean to change the subject and make this about me, Gabe. I don't know why Sasha broke up with you," Max said insistently, "but you have to win her back. You guys are great together."

Gabe shook his head. "That ship has sailed. Literally. She told me if I took my clients out last Wednesday instead of going with her to see the interior designer, we were done."

"That doesn't sound like Sasha at all," Celia said, pressing a hand to her chest as if that might soothe the ache.

Gabe's face jerked up, fury in his eyes. "That's what happened, Mom."

She patted his hand. "Gabe. I wasn't calling you a liar, only saying that it sounds out of character for her." Then a new thought hit her. "Where have you been sleeping?" Gabe had moved out of his own apartment last year to move into the cute little cottage Sasha had inherited from her grandmother.

"On the boat."

"Gabe!" His boat was a commercial fishing vessel, not a yacht. "You can't stay there. You should move in here."

"You know Dad always said once we graduated from college we were on our own," Gabe said. "'Life rewards those who work hard'," he mimicked his father's deep baritone. "'You'll never amount to anything by being a moocher'."

Max suddenly looked nervous. "Oh, he didn't mean it. Dad's all bark and no bite." She glanced around. "Where is he, anyway? Does he have a client dinner?"

"Yeah," Anna mumbled under her breath as she switched from water to wine. "If that's what the kids are calling it these days."

Stephanie's fork dropped to her plate as she reached across the table and swatted her sister's hand.

"Sweet, so if Dad's not here, does that mean you made dessert, too?" Max asked, her face brightening as she took a bite of her tuna melt.

Celia shook her head slowly. "No, I...didn't have a chance."

With every passing minute, it became more glaringly obvious how much she'd allowed Nate to take from her.

She'd loved baking. It had been a passion, one she'd shared with the kids when they were small. She could remember mixing brownie batter with Max and Gabe, flour on the tips of their little noses, chocolate ringing their smiling mouths.

At some point, Nate had made a comment about it being time to get "our pre-baby physiques back," but Celia knew "we" really meant "you". Nate was as lean and as fit as ever. Having back-to-back babies had changed her body, making her a little softer in the middle and a little wider at the hips. She hadn't even minded...

But apparently it had bothered Nate, and suddenly, instead of feeling content and sort of in awe at what her body had done, she'd felt self-conscious.

Why had she let him do that to her?

Gabe's voice jarred her from her reverie.

"Why are your suitcases at the base of the stairs, anyway?" he asked his sister around a bite of pasta. "Are you planning to move in or something?"

Max squirmed in her seat, making a face as she turned to her mother. "Maybe...?"

Celia wondered what in the world was happening. Had their entire family imploded? She shoved her plate away, her appetite gone.

"Dad's not going to allow it," Gabe said in a sour tone.

"He will if I sweet talk him a bit," Max suggested.

Gabe shook his head. "Never gonna happen."

"Well, it doesn't matter what he says," Celia said, reaching for her wine. "I'm the one who'll decide." Then her tone softened as she patted her daughter's hand. "Of course you can move in until you figure out what you want to do with your life."

Max's face brightened. "Thanks, Mom, and I already know what I want to do." Her grin spread as she glanced around the table, making sure she had everyone's attention for her announcement. "I'm leasing that property down on Maple Street. The one that used to be a dress shop. I'm going to turn it into a bookstore. I've already got it all in the works. Inventory on order, drawings for the space."

A bookstore? Celia had read that bookstores were closing right and left, but she bit her tongue. Surely Max had done her research.

"That property by the boardwalk? The one that backs up to the beach?" Gabe asked, incredulous. "You'll never be able to afford that."

"That's why I'm moving in with Mom and Dad," Max said in defiance, her chin lifted and her eyes gleaming. "So that I *can*."

"It doesn't matter what Mom says," Gabe countered, focusing on the mountain of spaghetti on his plate. "It ultimately comes down to what *Dad* decides."

Celia stared at her son in shock. Was that true? The years rushed through her head at warp speed, and she realized that it was. She could count on one hand the number of times she'd put her foot down and insisted on her own way, and if she were honest, all of those instances had happened much earlier in her marriage. She'd just acquiesced to Nate, because it had been easier than starting a disagreement or dealing with his silent disapproval.

How had she let things get so bad? Why hadn't she seen this before now?

Everyone was quiet, silently trying to choke down their food with the tension pressing down on them.

Finally, Gabe asked, "Okay, I'll bring up the elephant in the room. Why did you call this dinner, Mom? The last time you cooked both of our favorites was when you and Dad

55

told us you were selling the family home." He paused. "You're not selling this place, are you?"

Goodness, Celia hadn't even thought that far ahead. Would she have to sell the house?

There was a lot to consider, but one thing was certain; her kids were going through their own issues, and there was no way she was going to dog pile them with more bad news. She smiled, although the corners of her mouth twitched at being forced into the unnatural position. "I just missed you both, is all. I wanted to see my babies."

Max flashed her an adoring smile. "I love you, Mom."

Tears welled in Celia's eyes. She hadn't seen Max as much these past few years, but they'd always been close. Maybe it was a good thing her daughter was coming home. "I love you, too." She turned to Gabe. "I love you both so much."

Anna slammed her wine glass on the table with enough force to make some of the wine slosh out. At least it was white. "Oh for heaven's sake, Celia. You're not protecting them by keeping this from them. You know it's going to be gossip fodder by tomorrow morning. Better for them to find out from you than from Eva Hildebrand at the diner."

Granted, as a waitress at Mo's Diner, Eva was a natural gossip, but she was harmless. Surely she wouldn't tell the kids...

Max's eyes narrowed. "Mom, what's Aunt Anna talking about?"

Celia slowly shook her head at her sister, mouthing "no".

But Anna had never liked following instructions. She sucked in a deep breath and, turning from her nephew to her niece, said, "Gabe, Maxine, your father left your mom for the realtor lady."

Both stared at her in shock, and finally Max said, "The one who sold Mom and Dad this house?"

"A blonde tart with a fascination for silk and things that smell like the 1970s?" Anna asked. "That's the one."

Gabe opened his mouth then shut it.

Stephanie was shooting daggers at Anna. "Anna, what have you done?"

"What?" Anna asked, taking a sip of her wine. "Celia chickened out, so I took care of it."

"It wasn't up to you to tell them!" Then she added, "You don't have kids, so I wouldn't expect you to understand how to handle these matters."

Celia knew she should be irritated at Anna, too, but all she felt was relief. The secret was out… no more pretending.

She'd realized she was sick to death of pretending.

"I know this is a surprise to the two of you. If I'm being honest, it was a surprise to me, as well. But the most important thing you need to know is that I'm going to be all right. We all are," she said, forcing some facsimile of a reassuring smile. "It's going to take some time. I'm sure there will be questions and recriminations and tears, but we will get through it. Your father and I both love you guys very much, and I'm sorry we weren't able to—"

"Screw that!" Max shot back, pushing herself from the table and standing. "Dad left you for another woman and you expect us to just be cool with him now? Like nothing happened?" she demanded, her wide blue eyes full of indignation.

Celia let out a long sigh and tried not to let her kids see how close she was to falling apart.

"No, honey. But I *do* expect you to remember that he's your father and, while he did make some mistakes, he deserves your respect."

"Like he respected you?" Gabe asked, his angular face, so like his father's, a mask of fury.

"We had a lot of good years," Celia countered gently, toying with the nubby fabric of the table cloth. "This doesn't take that away."

"You should've left him a long time ago," Gabe said, his jaw flexing. "He always tried to squash you. You deserve better."

Celia drew back like she'd been slapped. She'd had no idea Gabe felt that way. He'd certainly never said anything to her about it in the past. She opened her mouth, instinctively intending to defend Nate, but then she stopped herself. She recognized that look on Gabe's face. There would be no talking to him now. His heels were dug in and that was that. She let her gaze flicker to her daughter, whose eyes were now shining with tears. Max was still processing, and Celia knew that nothing else she said at this point would make one bit of difference. They needed to come to terms with what had happened in their own time. Tomorrow was a new day.

"Is anyone going to eat that?" Anna asked as she eyed the triangle of garlic bread on a plate in the middle of the table.

Stephanie glared at her and Anna shrugged.

"What? No point in it going to waste."

She nabbed the bread and munched on it quietly while the rest of them pushed food around their plates. When Celia couldn't stand the silence another moment, she stood with a weary smile.

"Max, I'm going to head upstairs and put some sheets on the guest bed and then I'm going to lie down for a while and read before bed. It's been a very long day."

Gabe looked like he wanted to protest, but Anna shook her head and he closed his mouth with a snap.

"I'll take care of the dishes, Mom," Max said softly.

Celia thanked her and began walking toward the stairs. Stephanie reached for her hand and gave it a squeeze as she passed by.

"Love you, sis."

"You, too."

By the time she finished prepping the guest room a few minutes later, she was fighting tears again. She felt like she'd cried enough to be dehydrated by now, but apparently not. Tears were like pain. There was no cap, apparently, and even after you'd had your quota, that didn't mean there wasn't more on the horizon.

She padded barefoot down the hallway toward the bedroom she and Nate had shared, apprehension growing with every step. When she pushed the door open, she half expected to find Nate standing there. But the only thing waiting for her was the bed she'd made three days before and her sweet pup, Tilly.

Other than this weekend, this would be the first night she'd slept without Nate in decades. She crossed the room and lay down on top of the comforter, curling herself into a ball, face pressed against Tilly's fur.

For the first time in her adult life... No husband to share her joys and sadness with, or to cuddle with at night. No one to take care of.

Except for you, Cee-cee, a little voice whispered. *You have to take care of you.*

Now, to find a way to make sure that was enough.

Chapter Six

Anna stood back and admired her handiwork with a satisfied nod. Two hours and a lot of heavy lifting, but at least it was done.

"What do you think, Pop?" she asked, turning toward her father. "You like?"

She might not be a great cook like Cee-cee, but she had an eye for design, and the changes she'd made to the layout of her dad's bungalow were pretty fabulous, if she did say so herself.

He scratched at the grey scruff on his chin and frowned up at her from the couch. "What was wrong with the way it was before?"

What she couldn't say, at least not outright, was that it had been an accident waiting to happen. After Anna's mother had died, her father had refused to sleep in the room they'd shared. Instead, he'd started sleeping in the bedroom upstairs, something that had required him to climb a narrow staircase twice a day, which was an accident waiting to happen. When it came to physical health, he was a spry enough eighty, but with early onset dementia, he got confused and disoriented very easily. More easily than when she'd been back to Bluebird Bay just four months before.

The decline had been sharp enough to make her hands go clammy.

"It looked good the way it was," she conceded, "but Cee-cee, Steph and I talked, and we think that it's better if you try to do most of your day-to-day stuff on the first floor." She'd moved him into her and Steph's old room so he wouldn't have grounds to object.

"You three busybodies oughta worry about your own houses," Pop muttered, crossing his arms over his barrel chest. "I was at the diner yesterday for the Salisbury steak early bird, and heard through the grapevine that Nate moved out. With you not being able to land a man at all, Stephanie's husband kicking the bucket, and now this, it's a real fine how-do-you-do for a father, I tell you what."

Anna winced and raked a hand through her mass of sweaty curls. Cee-cee and Nate had split a week ago, but Stephanie had suggested they hold off on telling their father until the divorce proceedings were officially underway. Cee-cee had been only too glad to grab onto the excuse with both hands. They should've known a week was pushing it.

Red Sullivan was an all-around great guy. The kind to stop on the side of the road if a stranger had a flat. The kind to lend you his power saw. The kind to work eighty hours a week to ensure that his wife and children had everything they needed in life. Everyone in town loved him, including his three daughters.

But there was no question he had his head firmly buried in his bottom when it came to what he called "female matters". Old-fashioned, people used to call it. Anna called it supporting the patriarchy. She and her sisters gave him a lot of leeway because he was old and set in his ways, but times like these, Anna wished he was a little more mentally stable so she could give him a piece of her mind.

"Dad, Nate left Cee-cee because he's a spineless piece of excrement, not because of something she did wrong. And I don't have a man because I don't want one." She perched her hands on her hips and scowled at him. "I'm not even going to address what you said about Paul, may he rest in peace. That was just ugly. Stephanie is still grieving, so I better not catch you saying anything like that in front of her."

He had the grace to look ashamed...a little, but the mood passed quickly as fire snapped to life in his milky blue eyes. "She never comes around anyway, so don't worry," he muttered, sulking now like a child. "I told your mother we should rent out her bedroom."

Just like that, the anger drained out of Anna and she made her way over to the couch and sat beside him.

"Dad, Steph doesn't have a bedroom in this house, remember? And Mom passed away..."

She reached out and rubbed his shoulder gently as his fuzzy brows caved into a confused frown.

"Of course she didn't, she—" He broke off and swallowed hard, his throat working visibly as the memories returned. "I...sometimes I forget," he whispered.

Anna's stomach flopped and she nodded. "Me too, Dad. Me too. It's okay, though, that's why you have us. To help you remember."

She shoved aside the guilt that came with that statement. It wasn't like she was retired or had a husband to pay her way. If she didn't work, she didn't eat. Traveling was part of the job. She could only do what she could do. Besides, she'd committed to staying a little while longer, hadn't she?

"How did you get to the diner yesterday, anyway?" she asked, changing the subject to something less maudlin.

"I drove, how do you think?" he asked with a bark of laughter. "I can't very well walk there, can I? Almost three miles and it's hot as the bowels of hell out there."

Anna bit back a groan.

He definitely shouldn't be driving and Cee-cee had made sure he had her phone number on speed dial in case he needed to go anywhere. In fact, she'd hidden his car key weeks ago. He'd think of it sometimes and start looking for it, but he always forgot soon enough. Apparently, he'd had another key made in a lucid moment or maybe he'd finally found the one she'd hidden.

Anna made a mental note to speak to Cee-cee about what to do. She knew her sister wanted to allow him to live in the house he had raised his family in because that was where he felt most at ease, but it might be time for them to consider assisted living or a full-time nurse, however much he objected to the idea.

"If you need a ride, call one of us next time, okay? I don't want to worry."

"Worry about what? I've been driving longer than you've been on this earth, kiddo," he shot back with a wink.

"I don't mean about you," she said with a grin, "I mean about the other folks on the road. You're a speed demon."

His wide smile told her he took that as a compliment. Shaking her head, she pushed herself to her feet.

"You're too much, Pop," she said, pressing a hand to her aching lower back. "It's been fun today, but I've got to get back home and take a hot shower." Although she traveled the majority of the time, she kept a one-bedroom apartment in town as a home base between assignments. "There's a ham sandwich from the deli and a dill pickle for dinner all wrapped up in the fridge for you. Don't forget to eat it."

"Cee-cee will be by to remind me," he said, settling back against the couch, his eyes already drifting shut for his afternoon siesta.

"She won't. She had some things to do today."

Over the past seven days, Anna had been doing her best to take care of Pop so Cee-cee could figure out her next steps. She hadn't realized how much work it required on a day-to-day basis. Between making sure he ate right, got to his various doctors on time, took his meds, and socialized, it was easily a half-time job. It made her feel not a little guilty about leaving such a mammoth task to her sister.

Then again, Cee-cee liked to be in control of that stuff, so who was she to stop her? Besides, Stephanie was here to help. Anna would do what she could while she was here, and the three of them could reevaluate the situation once everything else settled down.

Already, though, Anna could feel herself itching to leave. This town was like flypaper. If you set your feet in it too long, there was no getting out.

She spared one last glance at Pop, already softly snoring, and then let herself out. Her back was killing her, but she'd told Stephanie she would stop by her office for coffee and a gab before she headed home. Although "home" was a stretch. It was more like a place to hang her hat and keep the thousands of photographs and negatives she couldn't bear to get rid of, but the water was piping hot and it was conveniently located next door to a shop that sold excellent matcha and even better almond croissants.

She made a silent vow to treat herself to one of each once she left Steph's, and ambled down the short driveway to her car. She paused by her dad's Buick and glanced over her shoulder before opening the driver's side door. The car had an emergency brake that took Herculean strength to muscle down once it was engaged. With one last surreptitious glance toward the front door to make sure her father wasn't looking, she yanked it up with all her might.

It wasn't a long-term fix, but it would probably keep old Evel Knievel off the road until he found some sucker to pull it down for him. She'd have enough time to work out a better solution with Cee-cee and Stephanie.

By the time she got to Steph's practice twenty minutes later, she was hobbling from back pain. Why hadn't she just waited until her sisters could come over to start moving furniture? At eighteen months shy of fifty years old, and too many nights sleeping in tents on the ground, she should've known it would bite her in the butt.

She hobbled up to the door, smiling with pride as she always did when she saw the sign there.

Stephanie Ketterman, Doctor of Veterinary Medicine.

Her big sis, a doctor. Given that their father had always pushed housewife as the preferred career path, and school teacher as a distant but acceptable second, it had taken a lot of guts for Steph to go her own way. She'd kicked that door open for Anna and her art, a fact that Anna never ceased to be grateful for.

"Hey, you," Steph said as she looked up from her desk, sliding the glasses down her elegant nose.

Her dark, wavy hair lay loose around her shoulders, and Anna had to swallow a stab of envy. How had she inherited this out-of-control auburn mop from their father when both of her sisters had gotten their mother's crowning glory? So not fair.

"What did you do?" Steph asked, her gaze arrowing as she studied Anna's posture.

"I went to Pop's and moved his bed," she replied with a wry chuckle.

Stephanie rolled her eyes and stood. "Geez, Anna, you're lucky you didn't throw your back completely out. Come on, I'll throw you on the table and work out the kinks."

"Also, FYI, he knows about Nate. Eva mentioned it to him when he was at the diner."

"That was fast," Steph said with a snort.

"Yup, no surprise there." Anna trailed behind her sister and gasped. "Oh my gosh, he's looking great!" she said as she caught sight of Shelley in his little kiddie pool.

The turtle's wounds were healing nicely, but it was more the healthy shine in his eyes that suggested he was on the mend.

"We're hopeful," Steph said, bending low to pat the turtle's head. "So far, everything is holding up great, but it's going to be weeks before we know for sure."

"Well, color me impressed. You and Mick really nailed it."

"I hope so. It would be amazing if old Shelley here could go back home. Now stop stalling." Steph patted the exam table.

Anna hesitated. "Am I going to be lying in llama spit or something?"

"No."

"Is it going to hurt?" she asked, climbing gingerly onto the table.

"Yes," Steph deadpanned.

Anna let out a pained laugh. Turned out, her sister's ministrations only hurt for the first few minutes. After that, it was nothing but relief.

"Whatever you paid for those doggy massage classes was worth every penny," she murmured sleepily when Steph patted her twenty minutes later. "My compliments to the chef."

She sat up and stretched in relief.

"Take some ibuprofen for inflammation before bed and you should be good. But don't keep pulling crap like that. You're not thirty anymore, Anna."

Once a bossy big sister, always a bossy big sister. The thought echoed her own, but she didn't want to dwell.

"Yeah, yeah. Hey, by the way, when I was at Dad's he told me he took the Buick out."

"Oh, boy," Steph said, dropping into a chair next to the table with a sigh. "Okay, well, better tell Cee-cee."

"Yeah, I plan to. He was really out of it. When I first got there, I found his cordless phone in the refrigerator, and then he was saying all kinds of strange things."

"Like what?" Steph asked, tucking a stray lock of hair behind one ear.

"Like, he thought Mom was still alive and that you had a bedroom there. And that you never come to see him."

Something flickered in Stephanie's expression, just for an instant, but it was long enough that it had Anna's eyes narrowing.

"Steph?"

"What?" she shot back, suddenly irritable.

"I know you've been busy this week and I was here to pick up the slack, but you go over there a lot when I'm out of town, right?"

"I don't keep a log of it, Anna, but I can tell you this much, I go over there a heck of a lot more than you do," Stephanie replied, her tone brittle.

Anna stared at her, nonplussed. "Right. Because my job takes me out of the country. What's your excuse?"

Stephanie lifted her chin, her hazel eyes going a deep green as her nostrils flared. "I'm a grown woman and you're my little sister, not my mother. I don't need an excuse."

"You do need an excuse because you're not doing your share. It's not fair to Cee-cee."

"And if you were so concerned about Cee-cee," Stephanie said in a cold tone, "you'd find a job here and quit finding excuses to run from responsibility."

"*Excuse me?*" Anna shouted. "What the hell are you talking about?"

"You don't have a husband, no family. Hell, you don't even own your own place. You're nearly fifty years old, and you've taken absolutely no responsibility in your life."

Anna stared at her sister in shock, then said the first mean thing that came to mind. "At least I can let go of the past."

Stephanie took a step toward Anna, her hands clenched at her sides. "Are you talking about Paul?"

"I don't know, Steph," Anna snapped. "You tell me."

Tears glistened in Stephanie's eyes. Anna knew she'd gone too far, but she couldn't find it in herself to apologize. Her sister had struck too deep.

Clearing her throat, Stephanie said, "You can let yourself out."

Stephanie swept from the room like a queen holding court. Anna considered chasing her and telling her exactly what she thought of being dismissed like some bumbling servant, but instead she slid off the table and grabbed her purse before letting herself out the side door. But as she walked to her car, she couldn't silence the little voice inside her head that wondered if there was some truth in her sister's words. Fact was, she didn't want to pick at this wound any more than Steph did right now. It would open a whole can of worms it was easier to leave closed.

Because once it was opened? She'd have to face the truth, and she didn't quite know what that was yet.

But something told her it was going to hurt.

Chapter Seven

"M om," Max said in exasperation. "I locked up Tilly for you. We need to go." She was dressed in her recently acquired daily uniform of jeans and an old T-shirt, her long dark hair pulled back into a ponytail.

"Just a minute," Celia murmured as she put the last of the cupcakes into the plastic carriers. She'd had to dig them out of a box in the garage. Although she'd never had the heart to get rid of them, they hadn't been used since Max was in high school. Celia had made ten dozen of her famous cupcakes for a bake sale hosted by the junior class. They'd asked, which had felt like a major compliment, and it had been for a good cause—a student had been diagnosed with leukemia and the junior class was rallying to help offset some of the medical costs. Besides, Celia had missed baking after Nate had suggested they cut back on the family's sugar consumption.

But Nate was gone, and Celia had spent the last week baking up a storm. She'd made so many baked goods that she'd resorted to giving them away, much to the delight of her siblings and friends.

"Mom. We're going to be late."

Celia snapped the lid closed on the maple bacon cupcakes, then stacked it on the container containing the pink lemonade flavor. "And you'll endear yourself to your new neighbors by passing out cupcakes."

Max opened her mouth to say something, then promptly closed it, giving her a forced smile instead. "Yep. You're right." She grabbed Celia's car keys as she headed out the door to the garage, calling over her shoulder, "I'm driving."

Celia headed out the door after her, balancing the cupcake containers and her purse. Her daughter was waiting in the driver's seat of the car, the garage door already open. As soon as Celia got her door closed, Max started backing up.

"Why are you in such a hurry?" Celia asked, a bit irritated at being rushed.

"I'm meeting a contractor who's going to give me a bid." Max backed the car out and took off down the road. "Everyone says Mick Rafferty is the best carpenter in town, but he's hard to come by, so I don't want to be late and lose him. Aunt Stephanie set up the meeting."

Celia's heart leapt into her throat. "Mick?"

Max swiveled her head to glance at her mother. "Do you know him?"

She and Mick had been friends in high school, and among her sisters, it was no secret that she'd had a crush on him. She was sure he'd liked her, too, but he'd never asked her out, even if he was friendly. Anna had cajoled her multiple times, trying to get her to be a "modern woman" and ask *him* out, but she'd never found the courage. Celia had gone off to college while Mick had stayed home to work with his father at his construction company. She'd returned to Bluebird Bay, but by then she was with Nate. Mick had never married, although she knew that he'd had several long-term relationships. She'd seen him plenty of times since she'd returned home, and sometimes they spent a few minutes catching up and reminiscing about high school, but they hadn't chatted in several years. Celia had done a lot of thinking about her life and the choices she'd made—the good and the bad—and she couldn't help thinking she'd made a mistake by ignoring her sister's advice all those years ago. She'd let fear rule her life, but she was trying to be brave now. Even when it was hard.

Celia realized she still hadn't answered Max's question. "Yeah," Celia said. "We went to high school together. Aunt Anna and Aunt Stephanie and I were friends with him, although Aunt Anna was young enough that she only knew him because of me and Aunt Stephanie."

"Oh," Max muttered to herself as she pulled up to a stop sign. "I guess that makes sense." They rode in silence for a moment before Max said, "You never told me how your second meeting with your attorney went."

Celia took a deep breath, her shoulders tensing up at the thought. "Your father has retained his own attorney and seems open to mediation." She swallowed. "He says he wants to get this resolved as quickly as possible."

"So he can marry *Amanda*," Max sneered, saying the woman's name in a snippy tone.

"Your father found someone he loves," Celia said carefully, not wanting to add fuel to the fire. "He's ready to move on with the new phase of his life." And Celia was ready to have him out of hers.

"Don't do that, Mom," Max snapped. "Don't make excuses for him. You've done that ever since I can remember. Just admit he screwed up."

Celia gasped at her daughter's bluntness. "Is that what you think I'm doing?"

"Isn't it?"

Was it? She could hear the truth in her daughter's words and Gabe had alluded to the same thing the night she—or rather, Anna—had broken the news. Celia had done lots of smoothing over when Nate had missed soccer games and dance recitals. He'd devoted a lot of time to building his business, but they'd all reaped the benefits. Celia and the kids wouldn't have had the nice house and things if not for Nate's hard work. Sacrifices had been made, and Celia had fully supported her husband's efforts. It had been a joint decision. "Your father worked hard to provide for us," Celia said. "I wasn't making excuses now *or* back then. I appreciated the sacrifices he made."

"Why aren't you *angry*, Mom? He *cheated* on you! He cheated on *us*."

Celia knew she *should* be angry, but after her initial burst of fury over him taking Tilly had burned out, all she felt was exhaustion. But she knew the process had only just begun. "Yes, he cheated on me," she admitted, pushing past the lump in her throat. "But he didn't cheat on *you*. He's still your father, and he still loves you very much."

"He broke up our family," Max said in a stubborn tone. "Which means he cheated on us, too."

Celia wasn't sure how to answer that. "I won't deny that he hurt me, or that I'm embarrassed, but he left *me*, Max, not you kids. He's still your father, and he loves you. I'd hate for you to give up on him because of this."

Max started to say something then stopped. "You're a better person than I am, Mom."

She wasn't. She fully expected the anger stage to return with a vengeance, but for now, she was still in the shock and awe phase, and thankfully it numbed her pain. For how long, she didn't know, but she would ride this wave as long as she could before the ugly emotions all broke loose.

Both women were quiet the rest of the way to the building Max had leased, and Celia had to bite her tongue at her driving, just as she'd bitten her tongue at the dirty dishes she kept finding in the sink and the presence of Max's discarded shoes in the living room. But a little messiness and aggravation was worth having Max around. Her presence helped fill the void in Celia's heart.

"Have you talked to Gabe?" Max asked.

Celia was only slightly relieved at the change in topic. She hated thinking about her son being in pain. "I've tried, but he always says he's too busy to talk then hangs up." She turned to her daughter. "Have you?"

Max shook her head. "No. He does the same thing to me." She paused. "I'm worried about him. Do we even know the real reason they broke up?"

"No, just what he told me last week, something about him missing an appointment," Celia said. "They always seemed so happy together, but I started seeing less and less of them, mostly because Gabe's business has picked up and he's busier than ever. Sasha and I have been out to lunch a few times to discuss her plans for the wedding next spring, but I haven't seen her in at least a month. Neither one of them seems to be in a big rush to explain what's going on."

"Maybe *I* should talk to Sasha," Max said, and Celia could see the wheels in Max's head kicking into gear as she started to formulate a plan. "Ask her out to lunch and see what I can find out."

"Don't push too hard," Celia said, "and don't say anything you'll regret later, in case they get back together."

"I won't," Max said with a grin. "I learned the art of diplomacy at the feet of the master."

Given her daughter's earlier statements, it could have come across as an insult, but the look in Max's eyes told Celia it was meant as a compliment.

When Max pulled into the building's parking lot, she turned off the engine and stared out the windshield. "Dad wants me and Gabe to meet him for dinner," she said so softly Celia could barely hear her. "He said he wants to tell us his side of things."

Celia felt a stab of pain to the deepest part of her heart, and she admitted to herself that she didn't want her children to hear *his* side of things. While she wanted her children to maintain a positive relationship with their father, she was threatened by what he might tell them, what grievances he might air. The story he'd told her was simple, perhaps reductively so. He'd fallen out of love with her years ago, but he'd stayed the course because their life was comfortable…until he ran into Amanda on the beach. Then one thing had led to another…

The bottom line was that a good portion of Celia's life had been a lie. Meaningless. And now she felt lost and empty inside, like a shell on the beach being pulled out to sea by tumultuous waves, then tossed back to shore, over and over again.

She'd let everyone and everything take control of her destiny. She thought she'd just been riding the waves. Now she realized the truth—they had sucked her under and she'd let them. Although she knew the time had come to climb out of the tide and make her own way, she didn't know which way that was, and it made her feel tiny and insignificant.

She'd lost her husband and her marriage and the life they had built. What if she lost her children, too? What if

Nate told them he thought she had become unattractive and doltish? What if he told them all of the reasons he found her lacking—and they *agreed?*

What if they turned their backs on her, too?

"Mom?" Max asked in alarm, and Celia realized tears were streaming down her face. "I won't go if you don't want me to. Gabe won't go, either."

A vise gripped Celia's chest. "Of course you should go," she pushed out.

Max grabbed her mother's hand and squeezed tight. "Mom, I don't want to hurt you. I'm not even sure I want to talk to him. I just thought it would be good to air it out and let him know how angry we are. Maybe find out where his head is at."

Celia's eyes widened as she tried to break the band around her ribs and take a breath. She shook her head, wheezing, "Of course. You deserve that. You should go."

"It's obviously upsetting you," Max insisted. "And that's the last thing I want. Gabe, too."

Celia closed her eyes and slowly dragged in a breath. The tightness in her chest eased slightly. "You need to hear his side."

"Have *you* heard his side?"

Celia glanced down at her lap, refusing to look her daughter in the eye. "No."

"Unbelievable…" Max muttered under her breath, leaning forward and resting her hands on the steering wheel. "The man's destroying your life and he's still making you feel responsible."

Celia glanced up at her in surprise.

Max turned in her seat to face her mother, her voice firm as she said, "Mom. Listen to me. This is *not* your fault.

This is on Dad. He left. *He* made poor choices. Nothing he says is going to change my mind about that."

Celia wasn't sure how to answer, but she didn't have to because Max abruptly reached for the door handle. "Come on."

Her daughter made purposeful strides toward the sidewalk, but it took Celia a moment to gather her things and follow her.

Max had already unlocked the door to the shop and held it open. "Go on," she said, waving Celia in.

Once inside, Max took the two plastic cupcake carriers from her and set them on the floor by the door. "We'd hate for poor innocent cupcakes to be harmed in the fallout."

"What?" Celia asked in confusion.

"Never mind. Come back here." Max snagged her hand and led her to the back of the empty space, barely giving Celia an opportunity to take it in. A clothing store had been the last business to occupy the space, and the previous tenants had left behind a few circular, metal clothing racks. Her daughter stopped in front of what had been changing rooms. One long wall embedded with doors jutted out from the brick wall. It looked out of place, especially now that the shop was empty.

Max dropped her hand and picked up a sledgehammer leaning against the wall.

"W-what's that?" Celia asked, taking a step back.

Max shoved it into her hand. "It's a conduit to your emotions."

"What?" Celia asked in horror.

"You're going to take that sledgehammer and slam it into that wall and pretend it's Dad."

Celia gasped. "I can't do that!"

"It's a metaphor, Mom. We all know you don't really want to bash Dad's brains in, but you need to tell him how you really feel, and since you won't do it to him or anyone else, you're going to do it to this wall."

Celia shook her head. "No. *I can't...* what will people think?"

Max held her hands out at her sides. "Who's gonna know?"

"We can't just tear down this wall," Celia protested, trying to make her daughter see reason. "You haven't bought this place—you're just leasing it!"

Max's mouth twisted to the side. "The owner gave me permission to tear out the dressing rooms. Now take a swing at that wall and tell Dad how you really feel."

Celia wanted to continue protesting—she was hardly dressed for demolition work in her linen pants and silk blouse—but the look in her daughter's eyes told her that Max wasn't backing down. Celia decided that she'd take a few swings to make Max happy. Hopefully, she wouldn't get too dusty in the process.

Taking a deep breath, Celia lifted the sledgehammer to her shoulder, then took a tentative swing, but it was harder to maneuver than she'd expected, and it barely made a dent in the wall.

"Come on, Mom," Max cajoled. "You can do better than that." Reaching for the sledgehammer, she said, "Here, let me show you."

Celia gladly relinquished it, hoping her daughter got this out of her system on her own.

Once Celia took a few steps back, Max swung the sledgehammer over her shoulder, slamming it into the wall with more force than Celia had expected, shouting, "This is for ruining our lives, Dad!" The head of the hammer made a satisfying hole in the sheetrock.

Tears unexpectedly sprang to Celia's eyes, but even more surprising was the tiny desire to wield that sledgehammer herself.

What on earth had gotten into her?

Max handed it to Celia. "Your turn."

Celia took the hammer willingly this time, hefting it over her shoulder. She swung it with more force than before. "I can't believe you left me for Amanda Meadows!" Her hole was smaller than Max's, but it had felt good—great, actually.

"Good, Mom!" Max shouted enthusiastically. "Do it again."

Feeling strangely empowered, Celia swung the hammer again. "I can't believe you tried to steal my dog!" She made another larger hole close to her first.

"What?" Max asked in disbelief. "*He tried to steal Tilly?*"

"Not now, Max," Celia muttered, a sweat already breaking out on her forehead and her armpits as she heaved the sledgehammer again. "This is for lying to me for *years!*" Another hole, larger this time. "And this is for making me feel fat, even if you never outright said it!"

"Mom," Max called out in dismay.

But Celia ignored her, calling out grievance after grievance until the wall looked like a sieve and she felt emptied of her guilt and shame. She may have let Nate run her life for the last thirty years, but Celia was taking charge of the next thirty and more. She continued destroying the wall, although she'd shifted from airing her grievances to announcing what she intended to do to improve things.

"I'm going to start putting my feelings first!" *Slam.*

"I'm going to stop worrying about what everyone thinks!" *Slam.*

"I'm going to bake every day because it makes me happy!" An extra hard *slam.*

Celia's energy was running out, her chest heaving for air, and her arms felt like rubber bands. She would pay for this tomorrow, but she had one last swing in her and she intended to make it count.

"And finally," she said, under her breath so that Max couldn't hear, "I'm going to love me, even if Nate doesn't." She heaved the sledgehammer with one last swing, crashing it through the wall so deeply, it became embedded.

She took a step back, wiping the sweat from her brow, and turned to her stunned daughter.

"What?" Celia asked, trying not to sound smug. "Didn't think I had it in me?"

Max blinked, then seemed to shake out of her stupor. "No, actually. That took me completely by surprise." But then her eyes shifted past Celia, toward the front door of the shop.

She froze, stomach dropping. Someone was behind her. Oh, dear heavens. She spun around, her shoulder and back already aching.

Mick Rafferty stood there, mouth open like it was on a broken hinge, but once she faced him, he quickly shut it and a twinkle lit his eyes. "You're doing part of my work for me. Maybe I should put you on the payroll."

Of all people to witness her meltdown...but then she realized he of all people wouldn't find it so surprising, after all. He'd known her in high school, before Nate had taught her to care about appearances. She propped a hand on her hip, and instantly regretted it when pain shot through her shoulder. But she ignored it and said, "I might take you up on it. I'm in the job market now, you know."

Some of his merriment faded. "So I heard."

"From my outburst?" she asked, suddenly ready for a confrontation.

"No," he said. "From Eva Hildebrand at the diner. For what it's worth, I'm sorry you're going through this."

From what Anna had told her, Eva had already broke the news to Pop, so it should come as no surprise that she was telling others, too. The thought of people gossiping about her deflated some of her newfound confidence, but then she decided to heck with it. She was in the middle of a divorce, there was no hiding it. Besides, Nate had left her. She had nothing to be ashamed of.

Celia lifted her chin. "Well, if you'll excuse me, I have some cupcakes to pass out." She walked past him to pick up her cupcake carriers, while Max watched in amused fascination.

Celia groaned as she stood, her purse over her shoulder and a carrier in each hand, telling herself she needed to take ibuprofen sooner rather than later.

"Ice it," Mick said, walking toward the front door to intercept her. "Most people use heat, but ice is better." A slow grin spread across his face. "Trust me, I know this personally now."

"Getting old sucks," Celia said. "Everything falls apart—our relationships. Our bodies."

His grin spread, but something else warmed his eyes. "Maybe. But not all change is bad. Sometimes it's what we need to make room for the next phase of our lives."

He was right. Celia felt a burden lift off her shoulders. She glanced up at him, giving him a playful look. "I guess time will tell."

He gave a slight nod. "That it will." Then he stepped back and pushed the door open so she could walk out. But as she passed, he leaned in and whispered, "I'm happy to see you got your fire back, Cee-cee."

She turned to him, so close she could smell the spring-freshness of his shampoo. She held his gaze for just a moment as she said, "Me too." Then she walked out the door.

Chapter Eight

By the time Celia got back to the shop after delivering her goodies, Mick was gone and Max was waiting by the door with a broad smile.

"He's going to do it!" her daughter said, practically shaking with excitement. "He's got so many great ideas. We're going to do a reading nook in the corner with a custom coffee table in the middle. There'll be built-ins along the back wall, plus two rows of stand-alone book shelves in the middle. He even offered me the ones he has in his basement. He's going to refinish them for me so they look as good as new!"

Max's joy was infectious and Celia took both her hands and squeezed. "That sounds so great. If anyone can make it look good, Mick can. He finished Aunt Stephanie's and Uncle Paul's basement and it came out gorgeous."

"Agreed!" Max said, sweeping Celia out the exit into the balmy summer air and locking the door behind them. "Anyway, your high school connection really came in handy, because he's willing to do it for a song. Said this town needs some more female-owned businesses and he's happy to help an old family friend."

Celia's heart warmed at the sweet gesture. She knew Mick was a hot commodity. In fact, Nate had been trying to get him to do some work for his real estate offices, but Mick had always passed, saying he was too busy.

Interesting how his schedule had suddenly cleared up.

She made a mental note to send him a whole box of cupcakes in thanks.

Speaking of which… "Well, I know you were embarrassed about me going around and introducing myself with baked goods, but the gesture couldn't have been better received." She held up the now-empty carriers and shook them with a chuckle. "They cleaned me out. And once Mr. Bonomo at the florist shop took a bite of his, he told me I can have fresh flowers every week if I'm willing to do a trade with him. The whole plaza is really excited about the book store."

"Me too," Max said, beaming.

So she brought a little clutter into the house. Seeing her happy made Celia's heart feel ten pounds lighter.

"Have I told you I'm proud of you?" she asked as they made their way to the car. "For taking a chance? For believing in yourself enough to give up the sure thing for the maybe? I couldn't have done it at your age. I wasn't brave like you are."

Max stopped in her tracks and sent Celia a long look over the roof of the car.

"But you are now, Mom. And if you'd just stop putting yourself down, I think you'd find that you're capable of miracles. You were a great mother and a great wife. Now find out what you're great at for you, and put that same energy into it. I'll be your biggest fan."

Celia's throat went tight, and for the first time since this mess with Nate, she nearly wept tears of gratitude.

"Thanks, baby."

They climbed into the car and rolled down the windows, letting in the breeze. Just as she was fastening her seatbelt, her phone chimed.

She tugged it from her purse as Max started the car.

Pop.

She bit back a sigh and pressed the receive button. "Hey, Pop, how are you today?"

"I can't find my comb. Did you put it away somewhere?" he demanded accusingly. "You know I hate when you put my stuff away. I leave it where I can find it, and now I look like some sort of Chia pet. Can't go to the diner looking like this."

"Your comb is in the medicine cabinet in the bathroom," she said patiently as Max pulled onto the main road and started driving. "And you're not to go to the diner alone anymore, remember? You either need to get a ride from Phil and Stella or call me to take you."

His long, stony silence spoke louder than words, but Pop wasn't the type to let his displeasure go unspoken.

"So you're telling me if a grown man wants some pancakes he has to sit around and wait until someone can babysit him?"

Her patience started to fray and she bit back a groan. "No. What I'm telling you is that if you try to drive alone, eventually, you're going to kill someone and wind up in jail. Do you think they have pancakes in jail, Pop?" she demanded, biting back a smile at Max's guffaw.

He must've been as surprised as her daughter, because she could almost hear his gears working.

"I suppose not. I just think I should be able to go where I please," he said finally, his tone more congenial now and even a little wistful in a way that made Celia want to wrap her arms around him and give the stubborn old goat a squeeze.

"I think so, too. And if you didn't forget things sometimes, I wouldn't stop you. I just don't want you to get hurt, Dad," she said softly. "I love you."

The silence stretched between them until finally he let out a harrumph. "Fine. I'll stay home. But if you're worried about my health then you should plan to bring dinner by later. Your baby sister brought over something she insisted was a pork chop for me to heat up, but I'm pretty sure she pried it off the bottom of a work boot. There's a side of potato salad that looks like someone already ate out of it. If that ain't the death of me, it's safe to say I'm invincible."

Oh, Anna, bless her heart.

"At least she tried, Dad."

"You wouldn't say that about a surgeon, would you?" he quipped with a belly laugh at his own joke.

"Anna isn't a professional cook, so that's not relevant, but either way, I promise to bring something more appetizing over. If you're nice, I might even whip you up the pancakes you're craving."

"I'm nice," he said, his tone sweet as pie now.

"Okay, I'll see you at five, then. Love you, Pop."

He disconnected without replying and she dropped the phone back into her bag, looking out the window in surprise.

"Why are we here?"

Celia had been so distracted on the phone with her father, she hadn't realized that Max had pulled into a strip mall with Max's favorite clothing store in it.

"We are here to get you some new clothes," Max said in a tone that brooked no argument.

Old Celia might have let that stop her, but new Celia wanted answers.

"New clothes for what? I have tons of nice clothes," she said, gesturing to her linen pants and silk blouse. "Plus, I'm on a budget now. I have no idea what's going to happen at mediation or what my monthly bills will be once we decide what to do with the house and all."

"I'm buying." Celia protested instantly, but Max shut her down with a wave of her hand. "No arguing. I've got a lot of money saved up. You haven't let me pay for a single thing since I got to the house, and if you won't take a little something for rent or even groceries, I'm going to treat you once in a while. That's that, Mom. And as for your clothes, they're gorgeous. You have impeccable taste, but who dresses like that anymore unless they're going to a business meeting? You and Maria Shriver, maybe?"

Celia wanted to argue, but she surprised herself by laughing instead. "You have such an eloquent way of putting things, Max. Sometimes I wonder if you weren't meant to be Anna's child, and when she opted not to have kids, God gave you to me instead."

Max preened as she turned off the ignition. "There are worse things than being like Aunt Anna."

"Agreed," Celia said, taking off her seatbelt.

"I could be like Pop," Max said with a gasp of mock dismay.

"Lord help us all."

"I could go over there more, you know. Give you a break?" Max said, a guilty flush washing over her face.

"It's not your responsibility, Max. Your aunts and I will take care of him. He doesn't want to be a burden on you or anyone else, so when your heart leads you to go there, do it. Setting yourself up with a visit is great, too, but you need to focus most of your energy on getting the bookshop up and running."

Max nodded and shoved the car door open, shooting Celia a sly smile. "I can't wait to get in that dressing room. You'll be my human Barbie doll." She cackled maniacally as she rubbed her hands together.

For the first time, Celia felt a stab of apprehension. What, exactly, had she gotten herself into?

Ninety minutes and four shopping bags later, Celia and a breathless Max paused at the counter of the coffee shop to put in their order.

"Two iced lattes and a black and white cookie," Max said. Celia insisted on paying, and as soon as she did, Max dragged her over to two comfy armchairs against the wall. They flopped down with a shared sigh, although this was a *contented* sigh.

Celia mulled over the day and couldn't deny the glow she felt deep inside, like the first blush of a new sunrise. At first, she'd only gone along with the surprise shopping excursion to please Max and keep her from feeling like she wasn't pulling her weight at the house. Surprisingly, it had been Celia who hadn't wanted to stop because she was having so much fun.

She glanced down at the buttery soft, camel-colored ballet flats and stretch skinny jeans she'd insisted on wearing out of the store and sighed. So much more comfy than those stupid linen pants. She reached down and ran a hand over the front of her triple-washed, navy cotton T-shirt that slipped off one shoulder to bare just a hint of clavicle. And this wasn't even her favorite outfit. She had five more that she loved just as much.

She hadn't known she could feel put together and, yeah, even a little sexy in comfy jeans. She could only imagine Nate's shock if he ever found out that she'd bought a pair of men's boxers and a camisole to sleep in. Even the thought made her lips twitch.

"I'm a convert," she admitted to Max with a wry smile as the barista dropped off their drinks and cookie to share. "I feel like I was in some sort of trance after a witch gave me a poison apple or something."

"And I was your Princess Charming and kissed you awake," Max said, leaning in and mashing her lips against Celia's cheek with a loud *smack*. "You look so relaxed and pretty. Seriously, ten years younger, Mom."

Celia flushed with pleasure and took a sip of her latte. The creamy, sweet treat slid down her throat and she sighed in pleasure. Life with Nate had been so regimented. So barren of the little joys that she couldn't help but marvel at them still. She broke off the white half of the cookie and gave the chocolate half to her daughter—a ritual they'd shared when she was little.

She'd already gained two pounds since Nate had left, but she refused to feel guilty. So long as she fed her body nutritious foods most of the time and exercised for health and longevity, she would no longer deprive herself of delicious treats.

Max glanced at her watch and looked back at Celia, a little of the light fading from her eyes.

"Um, Mom…"

Celia snapped back to the present and looked at the clock on the wall. "Oh, my, you've got to get ready for your dinner with your dad!" she said, setting her cup down with a clatter. "I didn't even notice how late it had gotten. You should still have time to shower and change before you leave to meet him."

"Actually, he said the parking at La Trattoria is a bear so there's no point taking two cars. He was going to pick me up, but I'll tell him no if that's a problem," Max hurried to add before Celia cut in.

"Nope. Not a problem for me. He's your dad, sweetie, and it's still his house, too, for the time being. I'm going to have to see him eventually."

Granted, she'd hoped it wouldn't be quite so soon.

"That's good of you, Mom. I'll run out when I hear him pull in, okay?"

"Whatever is easiest for you."

Maybe she'd spend some more time at Pop's house tonight to avoid a potentially awkward run in.

"A lot of women would've crumbled. I'm kind of in awe watching you go through this so gracefully. I knew you were strong, but..."

Celia wondered if her face showed how much those words meant to her after spending the past week beating herself up for being so weak-willed as to let Nate control nearly every aspect of her life.

"Thanks, sweetie," Celia said, clearing her throat. But Max's approval didn't take away the sting of remorse that she hadn't stood up for herself earlier. Gabe had freely admitted feeling the same, saying that she'd let Nate crush her spirit for far too long. Not exactly the sign of strength. She needed to talk to Gabe all of that—and also about Sasha—but so far that wasn't happening since he'd been doing everything possible to avoid her. Maybe he'd be in a better place once he hammered out his issues with Nate. She and Nate would start their mediation in a few days and hopefully that would move them all closer to an end to this nightmare.

She said a silent prayer that his time with their children tonight was one that resulted in some healing.

For all of them.

Chapter Nine

S tephanie was feeling out of sorts. After Paul had died, she'd fallen into a routine, her way of making sense of her life, stringing the tattered pieces of her heart together so she could function. Everyone had their place in her post-Paul world.

Or at least, they were supposed to. Everything was changing around her lately, and her new normal had been turned on its head.

She knelt next to Shelley, checking the cracks in his shell. He was healing well, and while he wouldn't be ready for release for another few months, Stephanie was already feeling melancholy about the prospect. He was a fighter, a quality she admired in anyone, person or animal, and she'd grown fond of him. She'd miss old Shelley when he finally went back into the wild.

Her phone rang and she was surprised to see it was Celia. They'd talked just the day before, and Cee-cee wasn't typically a daily caller.

"Hey," she answered absently, scratching the turtle's head before she stood. "How's Max's bookstore project coming along?"

"Mick has been a wonder," Cee-cee said in awe. "His craftsmanship is meticulous, and he actually shows up on time. Thanks again for putting in a good word."

Stephanie couldn't help laughing. "Mick's a rare one, that's for sure." She paused, then said, "What's up?" almost dreading the answer. If this was about Pop again…

"Just checking to see if you could get away for dinner or lunch this week. I know you're busy, but Anna and I haven't seen you in weeks. We miss you."

"You and I have just talked yesterday," Stephanie said, trying to keep the defensiveness out of her voice. Celia had kept her up to date about the divorce, and Nate—in his eagerness to marry Amanda—didn't seem to be fighting her sister on much. Last she'd heard, the divorce might even be final before summer was over.

"We're just worried about you."

"No," Stephanie said slowly, finally realizing what this call was about. "Let me guess—Anna told you about the fight we had a couple of weeks ago, and you're calling to put in your two cents. It's not my fault she stomped off in a huff."

Celia was quiet for a few seconds then said softly, "The way I heard it, you told her to leave."

Stephanie started to protest, but stopped because it was true. She *had* asked Anna to leave and they hadn't talked since. She knew she'd overreacted when her younger sister had quizzed her about going to see Pop, but she was a grown woman and she didn't need to answer to anyone. True, she'd said some hurtful things, but Anna had crossed the line. "Anna's overreacting, but that's her MO, isn't it?" she said, her voice short.

"Stephanie," Celia protested in a tone that reminded Stephanie of a kindergarten teacher reprimanding her class.

"Was I right? Is that why you called, Celia?" Stephanie asked with a sigh. "Because Anna's perfectly capable of calling and apologizing herself."

"Apologizing?" The word had bite to it, but then Cee-cee sighed. "Steph. Please don't do this. I need both of my sisters right now. United. Not bickering."

"Not everything's about you, Cee-cee."

Stephanie heard her sister's sharp intake of air through the line. "Ouch. Do you really mean that?"

Yes.

No.

Stephanie's emotions were all over the place, and while it was easy to blame it on perimenopause, she knew it was more complicated than that. It was a soul-deep pain that was tied to Paul and it wasn't going away.

She knew what everyone thought. It had been two years, for heaven's sake. When was she going to get over her husband's death? Celia kept urging her to clean out Paul's things, but she'd resisted. She wasn't a fool. She knew he was never coming home again, but it felt like moving his things out insinuated that he hadn't meant anything to her. That she could just walk away from all the hopes and dreams they'd shared as a couple. Paul had been the love of her life... her entire world. Everyone else had moved on without him, even the kids, and it felt like Stephanie had to hold on to his memory so he wouldn't be forgotten. All this stuff with Nate and Cee-cee had dragged up those feelings of confusion and loneliness. The self-reflection had been painful, and every time she saw her sister, her grief only deepened.

It made it harder, somehow, that Cee-cee was handling her divorce so well. She'd gotten pretty new clothes and had stopped straightening her hair, letting it go soft and wavy.

She seemed lighter, somehow, like she had some inner glow. And that only highlighted how little progress Stephanie had made in her own healing. Granted, a death was different than a divorce, but it still made her feel like she was failing.

That didn't mean Cee-cee didn't need her, of course, and she also knew she should make things right with Anna. Her little sister would surely leave town soon, and the last thing she wanted was to create a permanent rift.

"I'm sorry, Cee-cee," Stephanie said, squeezing her eyes shut. "I'm sorry I've let you down."

"You haven't let me down, Steph, but I *am* worried about you. When was the last time you went anywhere that wasn't your office or the grocery store?"

"I was just at your house a few weeks ago."

Celia released a small laugh. "That disaster of a dinner doesn't count."

Stephanie laughed, too. "Anna only knows one mode—blunt."

"Very true," her sister admitted, then asked, "What happened between you two, Steph?"

"Nothing," she said, feeling defeated. "I was just having a bad day." She definitely didn't want to admit to the ugly things she'd said to her sister.

"Reach out to Anna, okay?" Cee-cee said. "Life's too short to hold a silly grudge. Especially between sisters. My phone's about to die," Celia said. "So if we get cut off before I hang up—" And just like that, their call was cut short.

It was just as well. She wasn't fit company for anyone tonight. The stand-off with Anna could last one more day.

She finished checking on all of her overnight patients and the six dogs and one rabbit that were boarding, even though a veterinary assistant would be in to walk them in a couple of hours. With no other excuse for lingering in the office, Stephanie headed out to her car. It was after she'd turned the key in the ignition that she realized the true source of her irritation.

Anna was right.

Stephanie hated to admit it, but it was true. She *had* been avoiding Pop, and she knew she was shirking her responsibilities, but every time she was with him, anxiety washed over her. She was about to pull out of the parking lot when her phone rang. She nearly ignored it, thinking that Celia had charged her phone enough to call her back and continue her lecture, but she worried it could be a patient. With a one-woman practice, Stephanie was always on call, but thankfully, patients rarely called after hours. She didn't recognize the number, so she answered with her professional greeting, "Dr. Ketterman."

"Stephanie?" a woman said, her voice familiar. "This is Eva from Mo's place. I usually call Celia with this kind of thing, but her phone's going straight to voicemail."

"Her phone just died," Stephanie said. "But I'm sure she'll call you back after it charges."

"This isn't the kind of thing I feel comfortable leaving in a voicemail. It's about your dad."

Stephanie's stomach somersaulted. "What about him?"

"He showed up by himself for the Early Bird special. Celia's worried about him driving, so I made sure he didn't show up in his car. I thought one of you girls had dropped him off. When he finished, I asked him who was picking him up and he said he was getting his own self home. The next thing I knew, he was walking out the door and headed down Manchester Parkway."

"What?" Manchester Parkway was a busy five-lane road—the main road through Bluebird Bay. No one should be walking along it, least of all with dark clouds roiling on the horizon.

"I could call the police, but they might escalate it to a level you might not like."

"I appreciate you calling, Eva. I'll go get him."

Thankfully, her office was only about five minutes from the diner, so Stephanie took off, slowing down after she passed the restaurant, hoping he hadn't gotten completely confused and turned onto a side street.

A drizzle had begun to fall, and her windshield wipers kicked in. What if he didn't have a jacket? It was starting to get colder as dusk approached, plus a strong breeze was blowing off the ocean. What if he got sick? He wasn't a young man. She'd seen plenty of her older clients succumb to pneumonia in the hospital. In fact, her cat Smoky had belonged to one such client. Stephanie had adopted him to keep him out of the animal shelter.

She was still creating all manner of doom and gloom scenarios when, about a mile from the restaurant, she spotted him. He was standing on the shoulder and glancing around, a bewildered expression on his wrinkled face. She quickly whipped her car around and pulled onto the shoulder behind him.

The rain was beginning to fall harder, so she grabbed her umbrella and rushed toward him. "Pop!"

He turned around to face her, but his eyes looked empty. "Who are you?"

The words stabbed into her, but she tried not to wince. It was the first time he hadn't recognized her. "Pop. It's me. Stephanie."

He blinked as understanding washed over his face. "Stephanie...what are you doing here?"

"Getting you!" she exclaimed, moving close enough to include him under her umbrella. "What are you doing here? How did you get to the diner? Did you walk?"

His blank expression was back. "Uh…"

Did he really not know? Apparently, Anna hadn't been exaggerating about his condition. His dementia was worse than it had been.

Stephanie wrapped her arm around her father's shoulders, gently tugging him to the car. "Come on, Dad. Let's get you home and dry."

"I'm perfectly capable of walking home, Anna," he grumped, but went with her anyway.

"I'm Stephanie, Pop."

"That's what I meant," he barked, which actually made her feel relieved. He'd always called them by one another's names when he was flustered, occasionally throwing their old black Lab's name into the mix. Maybe it wasn't as bad as it seemed.

She got him into the car and cranked up the heat, then turned the vehicle around to take him to his house.

They sat in an uncomfortable silence while Pop stared out the window with a glum expression and Stephanie tried to figure out how to start a conversation. This was part of what made her so anxious around him. She never knew what to say. Although she'd spent a lot of time with her parents as an adult, Paul was the one who'd always known how to talk to her dad, filling the conversation void with everything from the Patriots to deep sea fishing to the changes in the weather. Without Paul, she had no idea what to say to him. She used to fret about it, so much so that she'd come up with a list of conversational topics before visiting her dad. But it didn't help. Things had gotten increasingly awkward, and her dad had ultimately caught on and confronted her, making her feel even worse.

So she'd stopped coming around.

It was wrong. She knew it, yet she couldn't help how she felt and her busy practice gave her the perfect excuse. She knew that her self-exile had made more work for Celia, but she'd promised herself she'd figure out a way to make it up to her sister. Eventually.

She pulled up in front of the house and started to get out, but her father said, "What are you doing?"

"I'm coming in to make sure you get changed."

"I'm not a five-year-old, Celia. I can take care of myself."

She almost corrected him about her name, but instead said, "I know you can, Pop."

"Then there's no need to go in. I'll see you in a few weeks." He got out of the car and ambled his way in while Stephanie watched.

She needed to find a way to fix this, but it seemed too daunting, just like a lot of things lately. Burying her head wasn't the answer. She knew that, but the actual answer seemed elusive, like a whisper in the distance that she just couldn't hear. If only Paul were here, he'd know what to do.

Drained and emotionally wrung out, Stephanie slumped forward, laid her head on the steering wheel, and wept.

Chapter Ten

Celia sucked in a breath through her nose and smiled. Blueberry lavender and Meyer lemon curd. Maybe her best concoction yet.

She glanced at her watch and ran a hand through her disheveled hair. Fifteen minutes until the next batch was out of the oven, which left her with just enough time for a nice cup of hot tea and to give Tilly a good brushing

She padded through the kitchen, bending low to breathe in the fragrance of the lilacs she'd picked up that morning, almost overwhelmed with the sense of freedom that rushed through her. Nate had hated fresh flowers. Said they triggered his allergies, which was strange because he never had allergies the rest of the time. He'd probably thought that simple touch of femininity would ruin his modern, sleek, aesthetic but hadn't wanted to admit it.

Whatever the case, he wasn't here now, so she had taken Mr. Bonomo up on his offer and her house had been filled with fresh bouquets ever since.

Not that it had all been roses since the separation. The situation with her dad was coming to a critical point. Steph had needed to pick Pop up by the side of the road in the rain last night. Some decisions would have to be made and soon. She just wished she could get her sisters to sit and talk about it. Every attempt was stonewalled by one or the other of them.

Then, there was Nate. They'd had as many arguments of late as they'd had discussions, but once he'd accepted that she wouldn't budge on a few certain issues—namely custody of Tilly and their vintage record collection, neither of which he'd ever enjoyed—they'd been hashing through things pretty quickly. All they had to decide was what they were doing with the house and then they could sign the agreement and make it official.

The house.

Celia looked around her with a sigh and rubbed at the bridge of her nose as she tried to think. The gourmet kitchen was grand. A cook's dream. But did she really need all this space?

"You're going to be the death of me with these, Mom," Max said as she passed by Celia and pecked her on the cheek before nabbing one of the finished cupcakes cooling on the rack.

"Those aren't even frosted yet, sweetie," Celia protested with a chuckle.

"Exactly. Which is how I get away with lying to myself and calling it a breakfast muffin. Don't mess with my rationalization techniques," Max quipped before biting in.

She let out a groan and gave Celia a thumbs up.

"Top three for sure," she said around a mouthful of cake.

Celia busied herself with the kettle, letting the glow of her daughter's compliment settle over her.

Right up there with brownie batter marshmallow and pistachio cherry. Celia made a mental note to bake a trio of her top three to bring to Mr. Bonomo at the flower shop next week. He had a case full of glorious pink peonies she had her eye on.

Max munched on her "muffin" as she rifled through the fridge, taking out the makings for a sandwich.

"Heading down to the bookstore today?" While part of her still feared for her daughter—it would crush Max if the store failed—she really was proud of her. And maybe a touch envious.

"Yup," Max replied as she popped the last of the cake into her mouth. "A few more days until the opening and I have approximately seven billion more boxes of books to shelve, not to mention putting my early editions into cases."

Sounded like a back-breaking day ahead, but her daughter looked nothing but excited for the work to come.

What a blessing.

"Tea?" Celia asked as the kettle began to whistle.

"Nope, once I'm done making my lunch, I've got to head out. Mick is stopping by to drop off the refurbished shelves in an hour, and I want to vacuum those spots before he gets there."

Mick had really been worth his weight in gold.

Max put the top slice of bread on her turkey and cheese and then stuffed the sandwich into a plastic baggie.

"Don't wait up for me, I'm almost definitely going to be late," she said as she rushed headlong toward the door.

"Okay."

Celia dunked her tea bag into the steaming water and glanced around her now even messier kitchen.

"Max," she called, "you really need to—"

But her words were cut short by the slam of the door.

"No, really. You go ahead, I've got it," Celia muttered as she moved toward the bag of lunch meat and mayonnaise-covered knife, irritation prickling at her.

It was no big deal, in the scheme of things. It wasn't like Nate was here to pick and prod over every little crumb or knickknack out of place, but Celia liked a neat home. Moreover, Max was an adult now. Surely, she could clean up after herself.

After a long moment of contemplation, Celia set the knife and the turkey meat down. She didn't want to have some big confrontation. She and Max were getting along great and she felt closer to her daughter than ever. But she wasn't doing her any favors by coddling her and cleaning up her messes.

More than that, though? Celia had allowed Nate to take advantage of her. Yeah, he had pressed her, again and again, but she'd let him do it. That was on her, but she wasn't about to repeat the same mistake with Max. She loved her daughter too much to let petty resentments put a wedge between them.

She was still thinking about what to say when her phone chirped. She dug through her apron pocket and pulled it out to find a text from Gabe.

You home? I'd like to stop by if you have time.

Celia thumbed out her reply without hesitation.

I'm home and I always have time for you.

It had been weeks since his breakup with Sasha, and despite Max's efforts to get the downlow on what had really happened, they were both still in the dark. Celia had to hope Gabe was ready to talk.

The oven timer beeped and Celia pocketed her phone. She was sliding the next batch of cupcakes in, having removed the perfectly golden ones, when the doorbell rang.

She opened the door for Gabe, who stood waiting with a sad smile on his handsome face.

"You don't have to ring the bell, you know," she said, wrapping one arm around him and squeezing. She'd given each of the kids a key.

He returned the embrace fully, burying his face against her shoulder like he used to when he was young, for just an instant.

He pulled away, refusing to meet her gaze.

"Sorry I haven't been coming around. I know you're going through a lot and it was a garbage move on my part."

"We're both going through a lot, so I understand," Celia said with a smile. Even so, it helped to hear it. She'd missed him and part of her had wondered if Nate had said something in his dinner with the kids that had affected her son's feelings for her. Max had assured her nothing negative had been said, but the nagging doubt had lingered. "I was just about to take my tea up on the roof to watch the tide come in. Want to join me?"

He nodded and loped behind her as she led the way to the kitchen.

"Kettle is still hot, so pour yourself a cup. Chocolate chiffon with raspberries or blueberries?" she asked, gesturing toward the trays of cakes spread out on the kitchen island. The lemon blueberry ones weren't frosted yet.

"Yes," he said back, his mouth quirking into a smile.

She laughed and put one of each on a plate, and they made their way up the stairs to the roof.

She pushed out onto the roof-top widow's peak and took a deep breath, relishing the smell of the salty air.

It was July already, but it felt more like September today, with just enough hint of a nip in the breeze to make her glad she had her tea. The thought reminded her of one of Pop's many homemade state mottos.

Welcome to Maine, where the summers are cold and the winters are colder.

They each took a seat on one of the criminally expensive but super comfy chaise lounge chairs that she'd chosen in spite of Nate's objections, and sighed as she took in the view.

And what a view. A spit of sandy beach that splayed out on either side of the house, visible for five blocks in each direction, and miles of tumultuous, stormy blue ocean. Not like the calm, turquoise sea of the Caribbean, but wild, full of roiling waves capped in white. Craggy rock outcroppings and lethal undertow made swimming a sport not for the faint of heart, but that didn't stop her when the mood struck.

She snuggled deeper into the cushions and watched as an osprey fell from the sky, hitting the water like a stone before emerging with a wriggling fish in its talons.

It wasn't the beach or the house she loved. It was this view. Sort of like baking, it soothed her mind and fed her soul. Nate wanted the house, or at least she thought he did, but why should that matter? What about what *she* wanted? Hadn't that been the whole problem in their marriage...her putting everyone else's needs before her own?

She turned her attention back toward her only son and watched as he stared out at the horizon.

"It's not getting better, Mom," he said, his throat working as he pressed on. "Every day, I'm out there on the boat alone and I keep thinking, 'Tomorrow is going to be the day that I wake up and don't feel like an elephant is sitting on my chest.' But then the sun rises, and it's the same." He turned to meet her gaze. "How do you do it? How do you force yourself to go on?"

Celia took a minute to compose herself before replying. Partly because she wanted to make sure she said the right thing, but mostly because she was trying not to weep.

Her strong, stoic son was admitting that he wasn't okay, and it broke her heart to think about him dealing with that these past weeks on his own.

"My situation and yours are very different, son. Your dad and I…" Haven't been in love like that for years? Didn't have what you and Sasha had? Were never truly meant to be?

God, was that true?

Celia shelved the confusing emotions those thoughts brought on, vowing to explore them later, and focused on Gabe again. "Weren't like you and Sasha. At least, we haven't been for a long time. We were living very separate lives in a lot of ways. As he put it, inertia is a strong force. We liked one another well enough and we'd made a comfortable, easy life together. But being in love? I think that had passed a long time ago."

She hated giving Nate credit for anything right now, but what could she say? It was the truth.

"Your dad and I are going to be better, more fulfilled people apart. I didn't know it when he left, but I know it now."

She could already feel herself moving toward that place. Like a butterfly still in the cocoon, opening its eyes and peering out to see the big, wide world that awaited it.

"I don't feel more fulfilled without Sasha. I feel like there's a huge chunk of my heart missing and it's killing me," Gabe muttered, pausing to take a long pull from his mug.

"Then you need to try to get her back," Celia said simply.

Gabe barked out a harsh laugh. "Good plan, Mom. But I'd already thought of that. I suggested as much to her, and needless to say, she passed on the idea."

Celia watched her son's jerky motions, marveling again at how much he looked like Nate. But the resemblance between them didn't end with their looks. Gabe struggled to express his emotions, and she had to wonder exactly how he'd posed his suggestion. She'd run into Sasha at the grocery store the week before, and the poor girl looked every bit as miserable as Gabe did. Dark smudges beneath tired eyes, pale and listless.

She was nursing a heartbreak, no doubt about it.

Celia opened her mouth to say as much and then reminded herself that she needed to be here for him and listen, not try to fix everything for him, as was her instinct.

"I just can't believe we're throwing it all away," he said softly. "Everything was coming together. She inherited the cottage and I was putting in seventy-five-hour weeks to make sure we could afford every repair and all the bells and whistles she's always dreamed of. We were planning our family together. Now, in the blink of an eye, it's gone. I'm single, no family to plan, living on a boat alone."

"That's got to be tough. We still have space here, at Casa de Burrows, if you want to move in for a while." He and Max would spar but they'd muddle through it.

"I appreciate the offer, Mom, but I feel like I can't leave the boat."

Celia cocked her head and eyed him closely. "Why is that, Gabe?"

He was quiet for so long, she was starting to think he'd decided not to answer, but then he cleared his throat.

"If I move in here or get a place of my own, it's like admitting she really isn't coming back. The dream of us together…our cottage, our little family…it's over. And I can't bear that thought."

And there it was. The heart of the matter.

"Have you told Sasha that?" she asked gently.

Her son turned his devastated eyes on her and shook his head in chagrin. "Not in so many words."

"Do you think maybe you should? What's the worst thing that could happen?" Celia said, leaning toward Gabe and squeezing his hand. "Sure, she may say it's too late, or it may not help the situation. You can't be more broken up than you already are. No harm, no foul. But the upside is so, so good, sweetie. What if it opens up a dialogue and you guys can work on what was wrong and make it right? There is nothing stopping you but you. Let go of the fear. Don't think about the blow to your ego if you fail. Think about Sasha and what she means to you. Now, if I'm wrong, and you think this will pass and you're just going through a rough patch, that's fine. But if you love this girl, you need to try so you know you put it all on the table. No regrets."

Gabe let her words sink in, but Celia wasn't sure they'd made an impression until he set his cup down and stood.

"You're right, Mom. You're absolutely right." His jaw clenched and his eyes lit with steely determination. "I'm going to call her right now and ask for five minutes to talk. Then I'm going to lay it out for her. Tell her exactly how much I miss her and how empty my life feels without her in it."

She cheered silently and nodded. "Okay, call me and let me know how it goes when you can, all right?"

"Will do."

He was about to walk away when he stopped and grabbed the plate of untouched cupcakes. "Can I get a to-go bag for these? If she'll see me, I think Sasha would love to try them."

"Of course!" Celia stood and followed Gabe back into the house to the kitchen.

She was on autopilot, though, her mind someplace else. Why was that advice good enough to give Gabe and his situation and not good enough for her to take herself?

Because you're a chicken. You don't want to swing and fall flat on your face. Especially with Nate and the whole town watching.

Screw that. The time for fear was over. She was going to live bravely. Take the risk. It was time to take her dream and make it into reality.

Celia Burrows was going to open her own cupcake shop.

Chapter Eleven

Anna was starting to get that itch again. The one that told her she'd stayed in one place too long. Maybe it was because two days ago she'd just been offered a job in Portugal, photographing a pride of recently discovered Iberian lynx. What did it say about her that she hadn't turned it down yet? What did it say about her that she wanted to say yes?

But she couldn't leave, not right now. She could have claimed she needed the money, but it wasn't exactly true, and Cee-cee would likely know that. Anna had been compensated fairly well for her work over the years and she wasn't frivolous with her money. Her small apartment didn't cost her much, and often she received a stipend and lodging when she was on an assignment, especially when she shot in the wild.

No, she couldn't leave. Not after the recent debacle that had left Stephanie picking up Pop from the side of the road. He was getting worse and it wasn't fair to leave Celia with the situation, especially since Stephanie seemed to be taking a hands-off approach, for the most part.

And then there was the issue of Celia's divorce. Nate was being surprisingly civilized so far, and Celia seemed to be doing well, but Anna felt like she needed to stick around, just in case. Who knew when Nate would suddenly decide to stop playing nice? With Anna's luck, it would be the second she got on the plane. She'd already missed huge chunks of her sisters' lives due to her traveling, and despite her still unresolved beef with Steph, she wanted to be around more now for both of them.

But what to do about that itch?

It was heavy on her mind as she walked into Mo's to pick up some dinner for her and Pop. When Eva saw her walk in alone, she asked, "Ordering takeout?"

Anna smiled and nodded, shaking the water off her umbrella over the mat at the entrance. Eva had really done them a solid when she'd called Stephanie about Pop, and Anna couldn't help but have warm feelings toward the brash waitress, despite her (deserved) reputation as a gossip. Anna had been in enough lately that Eva knew her routines. If she was with someone, she was dining in, but if she was alone, she was picking up food to go.

"Grab a seat and I'll come take your order," Eva said, carrying several plates of food to a table on the other side of the restaurant.

Anna did as she was told, taking a seat in a booth next to a window that overlooked the rocky coast and the harbor. After a sunny week, the weather had taken a wet, cold turn, and the ocean waves pummeled the rocky shore. Today wouldn't be a good beach day for tourists—and the rest of the week would be no better if the forecast was to be trusted—which meant the shops would see an increase in business. Good news for her niece Max, who was having the soft opening of her bookstore tomorrow.

Many of the locals would complain because some of those tourists would just pack up and move to a location more suited for indoor activities. But not Anna—she thought the Maine coast was more beautiful than ever in the midst of a storm. It was this very coast below her that had inspired her love of nature photography, her hunger to capture the majesty of nature. She captured the rare moments few people got to witness in person. It might take her two months to get that one perfect shot, but she loved it. She *lived* for it, and now she felt tethered to this place.

Home or not, the shackles still chafed.

With a sigh, she grabbed a menu at the back of the table and scanned the offerings, even though she'd already figured out what she wanted.

She was lost in her own musings when she heard a woman say, "Have you heard the latest about Nate and Celia Burrows?"

Anna's head popped up, but she didn't turn around to see who was talking. She didn't need to. She recognized the voice, even after all these years. Maryanne Carpenter, although she was a Brown now, on her second marriage, last Anna had heard. She'd had it out for Anna since high school, and as adults she'd seemed to resent the crap out of Celia's seemingly perfect marriage and even more perfect house, although Celia, bless her, didn't seem to notice. The witch must be eating this news up.

"I heard the entire family has lost their *minds*," another woman said, a voice Anna also recognized. Maryanne's best friend, Heather White. White had been her maiden name, but Anna wasn't sure if she'd ever married. Not that she cared. The two had formed their own mean girl pack back in high school and they'd never cared for the Sullivan girls. The feeling was mutual. But the Sullivan girls had grown up and left all that foolishness behind them. Turned out Maryanne and Heather hadn't gotten beyond anything.

"You know that's right," Maryanne said. "Celia's son has been living on his boat, and trust me, it's *not* a yacht. It's a deep sea fishing boat. Can you imagine?"

"He was engaged to that Posey girl," Heather said. "Sasha? I heard she's not wearing her ring anymore, and it all started when Celia's son wanted to take control of that house the poor girl inherited from her grandmother after her heart attack, God rest her soul."

Anna clenched her hand into a fist, resisting the urge to jump into the middle of the conversation and put it to a halt. Celia would be proud of Anna's decision to stay in her seat—less so of her reason for doing so. She was only remaining out of sight so she could hear what else the two women had to say.

"And their daughter…Max. She got fired from her job in Portland then convinced poor Celia to raid her and Nate's retirement fund to start up that… *bookstore*." She said the word as though it was synonymous with "devil's lair".

What in the world? Anna couldn't fathom where these crazy rumors had come from, but she was done listening. She started to get out of her seat when Eva popped into view, catching her off guard.

"Ready to order?"

Anna gasped and placed her hand on her chest, trying to catch her breath. "Eva, you scared the crap out of me."

Eva laughed. "You've taken photos of lions in the African desert. How could you be frightened of *me*?"

Anna leaned forward with a grin. "Everyone worth their salt knows you're the true power in this town. *Everyone* should fear you."

A slow grin spread across Eva's face. "Good to see someone recognizes it. Just for that, I'm gonna throw in a couple of slices of pie, on the house." She popped her hip. "I take it you want the usual for you and your dad?"

The waitress at the local diner knew her exact order. Anna knew what that meant: she was a regular now. She glanced down at the menu she hadn't needed, her heart sinking at the reminder of how much she'd become mired in the mundaneness of an ordinary life. A life she'd sworn she'd never have. "No, make mine a fried chicken sandwich...and fries."

Fried food? Anna avoided most fried food, but if she was sinking so low as to eat something she didn't even want just to prove how *not* entrenched she was in this town, maybe she should consider taking that Portugal job after all...

"Sure thing," Eva said as she wrote the order down. She glanced up, her smile spreading as she looked at someone behind Anna. "Hey, Beckett. You here to place a to-go order, too?"

"Yep," a male voice replied, getting louder as the speaker approached them. "The weather's got me working nonstop today."

"Your usual?" Eva asked, her pen hovering over the notepad.

"Yep."

Eva glanced around the diner with a frown. "Sorry I can't offer you a seat. We had a few open tables just a couple of minutes ago, but the rain's driving everyone inside."

"I can just wait in the truck," the rugged voice said.

"Don't be silly," Anna said, turning around to face the fellow takeout customer. She wasn't expecting the tall drink of water standing behind her. Chestnut hair that was damp

113

and unruly, looking like it needed a trim. The shadow of a beard and dark eyes. Anna was sure she'd never met him before. This guy, she would've remembered. She cleared her suddenly dry throat and smiled. "I've just placed a to-go order, too. We can wait together if you like."

His brow lifted slightly as he twisted the wet hat in his hand. "Are you sure it won't be an imposition?"

Anna laughed. "You might prevent me from committing a double homicide, so you'd actually be doing a good deed." She paused, scrunching her face as she considered it. "Although, maybe I'm wrong. Scourging our society of a blight might actually be seen as a heroic act."

Beckett suddenly looked leery and took a step back.

Eva laughed. "Oh, you two will make a fine pair. Sit, Beckett." Then she headed toward the kitchen.

"I promise I don't bite," Anna said with a laugh. "Unless you want me to."

What on earth had possessed her to say that? She'd already made poor Beckett nervous—and worse, she'd done it purposefully.

She'd learned long ago that she was unconventional. When her sisters were marrying and having kids, Anna was camping in the Sahara Desert and climbing mountain peaks. She'd always done exactly what she wanted, but she couldn't count the number of times she'd been asked about the kids she hadn't had. Why she hadn't settled down with a nice man. Nothing was more tiresome than defending her right to be herself, so she often took the offensive instead. She'd act as shocking as possible to shut the whole conversation down before it started.

But now, as she stared up into Beckett's wary face, she wondered if she'd gone too far.

Nope. Anna was going to be herself and anyone who didn't like it was free to move along.

She turned back around to stare out the window again, expecting that was the last she'd see of him, but to her surprise, he came into view and sat in the booth seat opposite her.

He was stoic as he watched her, as though preparing for whatever shocking things she might say next.

She held out her hand across the table. "I'm Anna Sullivan."

He nodded slightly as they shook. "I've heard of you. Beckett Wright."

She laughed. "I bet you have. People love to gossip about me in this town." But it was mostly harmless talk about her adventures. Anna secretly loved it most of the time.

He shook his head and glanced out the window, his gaze narrowing on the coastline. "Nope, I saw your photo of the Emperor Penguin colony." He turned back to face her. "The one with the dwindling birth rate. You captured photos of the penguins and their dead eggs." He paused, as though considering his next words, then said, "They were just birds, but you made me feel their sadness. Their grief." He swallowed, looking embarrassed. "Anyway, I've seen your work."

Anna stared at him, speechless for one of the few times in her life. But then she pulled herself together and said, "Most people don't pay attention to the photographer. They just like the pictures. I'm surprised you even remembered my name."

"*Like* the pictures?" he asked in surprise. "I doubt they just like them. Your photos move people."

Once again, she found herself floundering for a response. This rugged, stoic man, who looked like he rarely uttered five words at a time, had not only seen a set of her photos, but she'd moved him and he'd *told* her as much. She wished she had her camera right now, because he was one of the rarest animals she'd seen yet.

"Obviously you know what I do," Anna said. "What do *you* do?" She gestured to his wet coat. "You mentioned the weather was keeping you busy."

He nodded. "I drive a tow-truck. Beckett's Towing. Some of these tourists act like they've never driven in the rain before and I end up hauling their cars out of ditches and away from wrecks."

She gave him a wry smile. "Good for business, I guess."

He frowned. "I guess, but a lot of them have families." He shook his head. "They need to be more careful."

"I suppose it's strange," Anna said. "Your livelihood depends on the misfortune of others." As soon as the words left her mouth, she was horrified. What had possessed her to say such a thing?

She was relieved when he didn't seem to take offense, nodding in agreement. "Yeah." But he didn't elaborate, not that Anna was surprised. Beckett seemed to be a man of few words, but it was clear to her that he had a deep soul. She could see how his job would bother him, despite it being a necessary profession.

They were silent for a long pause, the hum of conversations and the clattering of silverware against plates filling the void. Finally, Beckett asked, "What are you working on next?"

The question sent a pang through her heart. "I'm not sure. We have a bit of a family crisis going on, so I'm sticking around to help."

"You miss it." His gaze held hers, and she was sure those rich brown eyes saw more than most people likely realized.

Normally, she would have dismissed the comment and moved on, but she felt like that would have been an insult to this man who had just bared part of his soul to her. So she bared part of herself to him, too. "Yes. It's so embedded in me that it *is* me. I feel lost without it." She paused. "I've been here longer than I usually stay, and honestly, when I'm in one place for too long, I start to get twitchy."

He nodded. "It's like the call of the sea. My grandfather was a sailor. He talked about it when he got older and couldn't go out on the boats anymore." He gave her a soft smile. "It was in his blood. Capturing moments of nature is in yours."

She couldn't help gaping. This man—this stranger—understood her better than even her own family. How had that happened?

"Beckett, here's your order," a younger waitress said as she approached their table. "Eva said to rush it since you're in a hurry. It's on the house. A thank you for your hard work."

He nodded solemnly and took the bag. "Tell Eva thank you."

The waitress headed to another table, but Beckett remained in his seat, his face unreadable. After a few seconds, he seemed to realize that was his cue to go. He slid out of his seat and stood. "It was nice to meet you, Anna Sullivan."

"You too, Beckett," she said, surprised at her disappointment that he was leaving.

He started to walk away, then came back and she was sure he was going to ask for her number, so she was shocked when he said, "There's a new bedding ground for puffins out on St. Monica's Island. No one lives out there and it's newly discovered." He paused, looking embarrassed. "Anyway, it's the middle of their breeding time, and it's only an hour or so up the coast, less than an hour-long boat ride to the island. You'll need to get permission, but with your portfolio and credentials, that shouldn't be an issue." He shrugged. "It's close to home, but it might feel like you're traveling again."

Tears stung her eyes. "Thank you," she forced out.

He smiled, but something about him still looked sad. "Don't mention it." Then he added, "Maybe you could sell me one?" His face flushed. "I'd love to go out there myself, but it's protected and I doubt I'd get a pass. So I figure one of your photos would be the next best thing."

She found herself grinning like a fool. "Yes, of course, but I wouldn't dream of selling you one. I'll let you pick your favorite."

He looked like he was about to protest, but instead he nodded. "Thanks." Then he turned and left.

She watched him leave, her heart aching a little, which was foolish. Anna had long ago given up on relationships. She'd never met a man who could tolerate her travel schedule. Flings were a better fit for her lifestyle, but suddenly she found herself questioning that.

What was going on with her today?

Anna saw Eva hurrying toward her table with a carry-out bag, so she pulled out her wallet, removing enough cash to pay for her food as well as a generous tip.

"Here you go, Anna," Eva said, sounding out of breath from her rushing around. "Tell your dad I put extra sauce on his meatloaf, just like he likes it." She winked. "Added it myself."

Anna stood and handed her the cash. "Thanks, Eva. You spoil him."

Eva's smile fell. "I admit to babying him more than usual. He's just not himself lately."

Which was why the Sullivan sisters had some hard decisions ahead of them.

Anna headed toward the door, fully intending to pass Maryanne and Heather's table without even a glance, until Maryanne engaged.

"Anna, well, hello!" she gushed. "So sorry to hear about Celia."

Bad move on Maryanne's part. Anna was out of sorts and looking for an outlet. Ho, boy, was it on.

She slid into the booth seat next to Heather, bumping her hip against the other woman's to get her to scoot over. "Yes," Anna said. "I'm sure you are."

Maryanne must've sensed the incoming drama, and her eyes lit up with fiendish glee. "Poor Nate. I hear Celia cleaned out their savings and gave it all to their daughter. What was the poor man supposed to do?"

Anna nodded, her serious face firmly in place. "Yes, that's exactly what happened, but you're missing some key details."

Maryanne looked shell-shocked that Anna was about to divulge some secrets.

"You see," Anna said, leaning over the table and lowering her voice, "Celia wants it *all*." Her brow lifted. "Nate has a pretty good life insurance policy, if you know what I mean." She glanced back at Heather, who was equally shocked. She nodded, but Maryanne continued to stare.

"In any case," Anna said. "Hiring a hitman's not cheap, and while the bordello Celia's running out of their house was raking in dough, it's still not enough to cover the expense. So she and Max opened the bookstore as a front." She waved her hand. "Sure, it's a bookstore, but it's really what happens in the basement that's paying the bills."

"What's in the basement?" Heather asked in a hoarse whisper, practically wriggling with excitement

"You read those Fifty Shades books?" Anna asked, glancing back at her, then winked. "That's nothing to what's goin' on in Celia's bordello."

"You're lying," Maryanne said, her eyes narrowed with accusation.

"Am I?" Anna asked as she stood. "Maybe I'm trying to drum up business for Celia's bordello, and what better way to spread the word than to tell the biggest gossip in town?"

Maryanne's mouth dropped open wide enough for a small bird to fly inside.

Pleased with her work, Anna stood. "You be sure to tell your husband Barry all about it." She tapped her chin. "Or is it Tim now?" She dropped her hand and shrugged. "Doesn't matter. I'm sure he'll be looking for a night of fun soon enough." She leaned closer and winked. "Tell him to mention my name and he'll get twenty percent off."

Maryanne gasped.

Anna stood upright. "You two ladies have a good night!"

Feeling smug, she headed toward the door, not paying attention when she rounded a corner and slammed into the poor waitress who had delivered Beckett's food. She was carrying a tray of soft drinks that upturned, sending the liquid splashing onto the occupants of the booth to Anna's right.

Horrified, Anna was about to apologize until she saw the drinks had doused Amanda Meadows, who sat across from an equally wet Nate.

Amanda screamed. "You!"

"I'm so sorry!" the young waitress gushed in horror.

"It's her fault! She probably did it on purpose," Amanda shrieked, pointing to Anna, then she turned on Nate. "Why can't we stay dry with your wife and her sister around?"

Anna dug a few twenty dollar bills out of her wallet and tossed them onto the table. "I think you mean his almost *ex*-wife. *That's* to pay for the dry cleaning. This accident was unintended, but it's the best sixty dollars I've spent in *ages*," she finished brightly, then stopped at the door and turned around to face the occupants of the diner, most of whom were watching her in astonishment.

She gave them a little wave as she backed out the door with a sweeping bow. "Thank you, and good night!"

A mild applause broke out behind her as she walked out, feeling better about a lot of things. Cee-cee was likely going to kill her for all of this tomorrow, but at least she would die on a high note.

$\mathcal{C}$hapter $\mathcal{T}$welve

Today was the day.

Celia's steps faltered as she clip-clopped up the sidewalk toward the offices of Haverty, Campbell and Campbell. Today was their final day of divorce mediation. If they could get through just a couple more line items, they'd be done. If not, it was time to get a trial on the docket and do this all over again in front of a judge.

The past week had been challenging for her family, but she couldn't be prouder of her kids. Gabe had laid it all on the line for Sasha, something that hadn't been easy for him. Granted, they weren't back together yet, but they were speaking daily and seeing a relationship counselor, which was major progress. Gabe had finally come to realize he needed to find a balance between building his business and fostering his relationship with Sasha. He'd also realized that though he'd resented his father's workaholic tendencies when Gabe was growing up, he'd taken on those same tendencies.

While all that had been going on, Max had officially opened the bookstore. The drab decor had been stripped, the original hardwood floors had been refinished, and the brick walls stripped of three coats of paint. Mick had polished the wood stairs and ornate banister leading to a loft on the second floor. Last time she'd stopped in, Celia had felt cocooned and cozy the moment she walked through the front door, and there was no doubt customers would, too. Business wasn't booming yet, but it had garnered some buzz and Max had a two-year plan. Her kids' courage in going after what they wanted had inspired her to do the same. She was going to open her cupcake shop. There were all sorts of licenses to acquire, potential lease properties to research, and plans to make, but she'd dived into the work with gusto.

It felt almost selfish to take on such a time-consuming project given the situation with her father, but Celia knew from experience that she'd never do it if she waited for the perfect time. Pursuing her dream didn't mean she couldn't also be a good daughter and a good sister. It just meant that she was going to invest just as much energy into loving herself as she did the rest of the people in her life.

She reached the glass door of the law offices and slowed, taking a calming breath.

You can do this.

She yanked the door open and cut a path across the lobby, walking with a confidence she didn't feel. What was that saying Max was always quoting?

'Fake it 'til you make it.'

"I'm here for an eleven a.m. mediation case with Wendy Campbell," she said to the pretty brunette receptionist at the front desk.

"Sure thing, Mrs. Burrows, I'll let them know you're here," she said with a pleasant nod.

Celia's smile faltered as she watched the woman pick up the phone. The receptionist had said 'they,' which meant Nate and his lawyer were already here. She took a surreptitious glance at the clock on the wall and frowned.

She'd specifically showed up ten minutes early so she wouldn't have to walk into the room with all eyes on her. Nate would have to come into her lair instead of vice versa. It was meant to be a power move that would give her just a teensy leg up, which she desperately needed. But of course, Nate had turned the tables on her. She should've expected nothing less. Power moves were Nate's business.

That was okay. She'd lose the skirmish so long as she could take the war.

"All right, you can go on back, Mrs. Burrows. They're in conference room B, first door on your right."

"Thanks."

The walk down the hallway felt a little like the Green Mile. Her legs shook and she cursed herself for wearing heels. It had been weeks since she'd worn them and she'd almost decided not to, just to make a statement to Nate. But she didn't want to let him control the way she dressed, even inadvertently, so she'd taken him out of the equation and asked herself what she wanted to wear today. The answer had been a crisp, white, linen suit with a coral-colored camisole underneath and camel-colored, pointy-toed stilettos because the outfit made her feel like a million bucks...so long as she was sitting down.

As she approached the conference room, she could see her lawyer, Wendy, at the head of the table. Nate, his lawyer, and someone else were seated to Wendy's right, their backs to the door.

Who the heck was th—

Blood rushed to her ears as it dawned on her. Amanda Meadows.

Nate had thought it appropriate to bring his mistress to their divorce proceedings. And his attorney let him? Celia pinched her eyes closed and swayed, putting a hand on the door to steady herself.

He's doing this to shake you up. Don't let him. Remember the end game here, woman. You got this.

Anna had given her a top-notch motivational speech on the phone just an hour ago, and she replayed the high points in her mind before pushing the door open and forcing a polite smile.

"Good morning, gentlemen," she said as everyone turned to face her. "Ladies," she added with a nod, insinuating a tiny little question mark at the end of the word as she met Amanda's gaze.

"Great, you're early, too," Wendy said with an approving smile as she stood. "We might as well get started."

Celia gripped the briefcase she was holding in one clammy hand as she rounded the massive oval table and took a seat directly to Wendy's left, directly across from her soon to be ex-husband. As she sat, her gaze locked with Nate's.

She was surprised to see something unexpected there…regret, or maybe an apology? She couldn't be sure, but as Amanda reached out to lace her fingers with his, she knew it wasn't Nate's idea for her to be here. Amanda's little physical display of dominance was tantamount to peeing on her territory, and it seemed so petty and silly, Celia almost chuckled.

Amanda was threatened by her, which meant Nate still cared in some way. The why of it didn't matter. If he had any affection for her, it could only help her case. She could parlay that and his instinct for a good deal to get what she wanted.

"We've been able to come to an agreement on most things, which is wonderful. There are couples who fight over lamps only one of them wants, out of spite," Nate's lawyer,

Benton, said. "We're on a great track, so let's keep up the momentum. We'll start with Nate's retirement."

"Their retirement," Wendy said with a tight smile. "Celia gave up her career to take the unpaid position of housewife and mother and raise their kids, during which time the two of them decided together as partners how much money the family could afford to sock away for their golden years."

Amanda looked like she'd just caught a whiff of the wharf at high noon, nostrils flaring. She opened her mouth to speak, but Nate gave her hand a visible squeeze.

"That's true," he said, turning toward Benton. "I know we talked about trying to go 75/25, but I've slept on it and it doesn't feel right. That money came from our family budget and Celia deserves her share when it's time to disperse it."

Celia's pulse fluttered as she blinked at him in shock. Wendy played it a lot cooler, shuffling some papers around and then pushing her glasses higher up on her nose.

"We'd have accepted nothing less, but we're glad you're being reasonable, Mr. Burrows. We'll get that added to the agreement. Which just leaves us with the house."

She tapped her fountain pen on the manila folder in front of her and cocked her head at Nate.

"You left the marital home while your wife was away, and she's been living there without you ever since. Clearly, you have no attachment to the place, or you wouldn't have abandoned it. Celia loves it and wants to keep it, but can't afford to buy you out. So what's the solution, Nate?"

No amount of squeezing was going to keep Amanda quiet this time. She yanked her hand from Nate's and shoved herself to her feet. "See. That's why I came. To give my testimony as a real estate professional. A house like that is worth a mint, and with the upgrades Nate made, it would command an even better price. He painstakingly selected every faucet, every piece of tile, every scrap of wood to create his dream home, and now, because he doesn't want *her* anymore," she hissed, shooting a scathing glance in Celia's direction, "she gets to keep it? That's outrageous."

There was no denying that the house was Nate's dream home, and Celia had let him take the lead, letting her family think it was what she'd wanted, too, but Amanda was completely out of line. Celia had kept her calm to this point, but at that, something inside of her snapped and she lurched to her feet and leaned over the desk.

"The fact that you think your presence here is appropriate and/or necessary makes anything you have to say null and void because you clearly don't have the sense the good Lord gave you. So, right now, I'm going to need you to sit down and shut up while the grownups talk."

Amanda's mouth opened and closed like a landed fish as she sank back into her seat, cheeks twin slashes of crimson.

Celia didn't celebrate the mini-victory, though. Instead, she set her sights on a stunned-looking Nate.

"I don't want the house." Nate drew back in surprise, but she didn't stop. She had to get it all out while she was on a roll. "I thought I did, but Mandy Meadows was right about one thing. It's all you. Every drop of gray and white paint. Every harsh line and cubist painting. None of that is me and I don't give a crap about the place. I was looking at comps and I know what it's worth right now. To my mind, that gives us about three hundred thousand in equity, give or take. If you give me a check for a hundred thousand right now and agree to take over the mortgage, it's yours." She met and held his gaze. "What do you say, Nate? We can get this all done today, nice and easy, and part on good terms."

All four of the room's occupants stared at her in total silence.

"Celia, honey, I think we should talk about this first…" Wendy began, her tone pleading.

"I'm sorry I didn't tell you before this meeting, Wendy. But I wanted to be sure, and I also didn't want you to try to talk me out of it. I know it's your job to make sure I walk away from this marriage with as much as you can possibly get me, and you've been amazing. But I'm done now. All I want is enough money to start my business and move on."

"What business?" Nate asked, a frown creasing his brow.

"I'm opening a cupcake shop in town," she said, crossing her arms over her chest defiantly, waiting for the lecture she knew would come.

Nate, bless his heart, didn't disappoint as he shook his head. "Come on, Celia. You know that startups in this area have a seventy percent fail rate and f—"

Celia held up a hand and made an obnoxious sound, like the buzzer at the end of a basketball game, cutting him short. "You're not my husband anymore. I don't need your approval or want your opinion. You can tell Amanda here what to do with her life. All I need from you is a check and a signature, and we're done here. What do you say, Nate?"

Benton tugged on Nate's arm and pulled him closer, whispering furiously as Wendy did the same with Celia.

"Don't do this. We can get double that amount in court," she said. "I never like to go to trial, but it's almost a no-brainer."

"A trial could take months. This is what I want, Wendy. I've thought a lot about it, and I'm sure."

"Okay, Nate agrees to Mrs. Burrow's terms," Benton said with a smile. "Let's get this written up and we can all move on with our days, shall we?"

The rest of the meeting went by in a flurry of paper and signatures. Nate was quiet and reserved, but Amanda was positively beaming.

Celia didn't care, though. She had one goal and it wasn't to make Nate or Amanda or anyone else miserable. It was to make herself happy. And, as she walked out of the office, check in hand, she let out an unladylike *whoop*! Her feet ached a little, and her heart was a bit tender, but she'd done it. She had the money for her cupcake shop.

She was on her way, and she wasn't going to let anyone stop her.

Chapter Thirteen

That's not a good sign," Stephanie said as she watched Celia struggle to unlock the front door to the fifth retail space they'd looked at in several hours.

"The lock's stuck," Cee-cee said, leaning into the door to put more leverage into twisting the key.

"Be careful or you'll break the key." When her sister showed no signs of backing off, Stephanie said, "Maybe we should just call this one a bust."

Celia grunted as she continued to try to jiggle the lock in vain. "But the back of it faces the ocean, *and* it's close to the pier. Tourists will pass it on the way to the hotels on the northside of town."

"There's obviously something wrong with it, Cee-cee," Stephanie said. "The rent's way too cheap for a business on the beach and this close to the pier. It's a prime location."

"Which is why it's a good spot for my shop," Cee-cee said, refusing to be deterred as she took a step back then tried to peer around the paper covering the front windows. "I at least want to see it before I cross it off my list."

"How many more places are on your list?"

Cee-cee turned to face her sister, frowning. "This is the last one."

Stephanie pushed out a sigh. They'd already looked at two places in Bluebird Bay, another in Montego, a tourist town about ten miles north, and two locations in Seal Point, a town fifteen miles south. So far, nothing had grabbed either of them. A realtor friend of Stephanie's had called while the two women were at lunch strategizing about their next course of action. There was a space in Bluebird Bay that wasn't officially on the market, but the owner had recently inherited the property and insisted it be rented out at a reduced rate to local residents with new businesses to foster the Bluebird Bay economy. The rent was so ridiculously low compared to the other properties they'd seen, Celia had practically run out on the lunch bill in her haste to pick up the key.

"Too bad Anna's not here," Cee-cee said. "She'd know what to do."

Stephanie felt horrible that she was grateful Anna wasn't with them. While she and Anna had both wound up apologizing to one another—she for questioning Anna's life choices and Anna for her harsh reponse about Steph being unable to let go—they still weren't one hundred percent right, and Stephanie wasn't sure how to fix it. Anna now expected her to spend at least two nights a week with their father, and she hated to admit, even to herself, that she dreaded it every time.

"Well, Anna's off with her puffins, but it's a good thing you have me because I also know what to do." She forced a cheerful smile, feeling like a horrible person for the inexplicable stab of jealousy in her gut. "We need WD-40. Do you have any in your car?"

Cee-cee laughed, standing upright and grinning at her sister. "Do I look like I have WD-40 in my car?"

Stephanie returned her sister's smile. "Fair point."

But in reality, it was the old Celia who would have worried about ruining her silk blouse if she sprayed a can of lubrication. Celia 2.0 had changed her wardrobe and softened her hairstyle. She'd helped her daughter set up a bookstore and was now opening her own small business. For all Stephanie knew, Cee-cee had a fully equipped toolbox in the back of her car.

"We can always run to the hardware store," Stephanie said, glancing around the busy street. "Or we can ask around and see if one of the other shops has some."

"Good idea," Cee-cee said, "wait here."

Stephanie waited outside on the sidewalk as her sister walked into the office next door that booked whale watching and deep sea fishing excursions.

She took note of the number of tourists passing her on their way to the cluster of hotels up the hill, their cheeks and arms flushed or red from a day in the sun and the sea. A few of them mentioned being hungry, and Stephanie felt a little burst of excitement. Her sister was right. Her business would be booming if she managed to nab this place.

Stephanie pulled out her phone to check for messages from her office. It was her scheduled day off, but she usually went in anyway. She could never bear the thought of an animal in pain, and since Paul and the kids were gone, she had nothing but time.

However, watching Cee-cee's transformation over the past few months had left Stephanie unsettled. Her sister had every right to be wallowing in grief and pain, but instead she'd picked herself up, dusted herself off, and changed course. After taking care of everyone else for thirty years, she was finally fulfilling her own dreams.

Still, no one could say that Stephanie wasn't living her own dream. She'd always wanted to be a veterinarian, ever since she was seven. She and her mother had found a nest of baby bunnies that had been abandoned after being rooted out by the neighbor's dog. She and her mother had taken the orphans inside and nestled them in a blanket they put in a small box. Every few hours they nursed the bunnies with eye droppers, then eventually lettuce and carrots before they let them go. Her father had grumbled, saying they were wasting their time raising the very creatures that would eat the garden, but her mother would simply smile, peck him on the cheek, and tell him to go watch "the game"—whatever sport was on.

It was her mother who had fostered and encouraged her dream of going to vet school, even when her father had insisted it was a waste of time and money. He'd changed his attitude after Stephanie had finished her four years of college and been accepted into a veterinary school in Minnesota. He'd seemed proud of her then, but Stephanie knew she would never have followed through if not for the continual support of her mother.

But while Stephanie was indeed living her dream—she still loved what she did—she also realized Cee-cee had a new zest for life that Stephanie had lost when Paul died—a *joie de vivre*—and it made her heart ache for something more.

Did that mean she was ready to move on?

If so, did it mean she loved Paul any less?

"Got it!" Cee-cee gushed, emerging from the store with the can of lubricant held in the air in triumph.

Stephanie laughed, shoving the distressing thoughts aside. "That was quicker than I expected."

"See?" Cee-cee said, removing the key from the lock with a firm wiggle and pull. "I have a good feeling about this place."

To Stephanie's surprise—she didn't believe in signs or luck—suddenly she did, too.

Cee-cee sprayed the lubricant into the lock then reinserted the key, and seconds later, the door opened.

Since the front windows were covered, Stephanie expected the space to be dark, but the back wall was full of open windows with a marvelous view of the harbor, and farther out, the sea.

"Cee-cee," Stephanie gushed. "It's beautiful." And it was, despite a few bad patches in the filthy wood floor, and the peeling wallpaper featuring drawings of loaves of bread and bowls of pasta.

"There's no place for a kitchen," Cee-cee said, disappointment heavy in her voice.

"There has to be," Stephanie countered. "This used to be an Italian restaurant. Remember?"

"That was *years* ago." Cee-cee frowned as she turned to her sister. "Did they tear it out? I can't imagine where it could be."

Stephanie pulled her phone back out of her purse. "Let me call Barb and see if she knows what happened to it." She glanced around the twenty-foot wide by thirty-foot deep space. "Or where it even was." A kitchen would hide the glorious view and cut the dining space in half.

Cee-cee nodded, moving to the back windows to take in the scenery.

"Barb," Stephanie said as soon as her friend answered, "I'm on speaker phone with Cee-cee. We're inside the shop. We love the atmosphere, but we're slightly confused. Where's the kitchen? Did they remove it?"

"Oh!" Barb exclaimed, "I forgot to tell you that the rent includes the basement kitchen."

Cee-cee turned around, her eyes widening.

"There's also an apartment above that's not included," Barb continued, "but it's available, too. Hasn't had renters for a good five years or so. The key for the front door opens it, as well."

"What?" Cee-cee gasped, excitement in her eyes.

She was scheduled to move out of the house she'd shared with Nate within the next three weeks, and she still hadn't found a place to live. While Max had found a small apartment a couple of blocks from the bookstore, Celia planned on staying with Stephanie for a couple weeks during her real-estate search, but the idea of moving twice was daunting.

"Thanks, Barb," Stephanie said. "We'll check them out."

Cee-cee was already opening a door in the back corner and heading down the staircase.

Stephanie found her in the grime and dust-covered basement kitchen, which had its own row of windows along the back wall, along with a door that could be used for deliveries. "A walkout basement. I guess it was built into the hill," she said, watching as Cee-cee made her way around the room and checked out the appliances.

"This would save me so much money," Cee-cee said, peering inside the commercial refrigerator door that had been propped open.

"If they work," Stephanie said, hating to be a killjoy, but wanting Cee-cee to be prepared if they didn't. They looked to be a half-century old.

"True," she said, moving on to the next appliances. "Three ovens... It might be enough until business starts booming, then we could add more."

"I love your confidence," Stephanie said with a smile.

Cee-cee looked up at her in surprise. "Do I seem confident? I'm scared to death."

"You could never tell, Cee-cee," Stephanie assured her. "You look like you're ready to take on the world."

A sunny smile lit up Cee-cee's face. Stephanie couldn't remember the last time she'd seen her older sister so happy.

Stephanie glanced back at the staircase. "But how will you get the cupcakes upstairs?"

Her sister frowned. It would be quite the trek to haul her baked goods up and down the stairs all day. "Maybe that's why the previous restaurant closed. Because it was a logistical nightmare."

Stephanie suspected they'd closed because the food had been bad. She'd never eaten here, but her friends' word-of-mouth reviews had kept her and Paul from trying it. She glanced around, then spotted a cabinet door in the middle of the wall. "Cee-cee!" she said, pointing to the wall behind her sister. "Is that a dumbwaiter?"

Cee-cee spun around and lifted what looked like a small garage door. "It is! I can haul the cupcakes up this way. And it's wide enough to hold a large tray."

Stephanie's heart was about to burst for her sister. This place was almost too good to be true. "I bet you could get Mick to rig something up for you so you can stack them, too. You'll need to fix up the upstairs, anyway, and he's the perfect contractor."

Cee-cee paused. "He's so busy... He might not have time to fit me in."

"He took on Max's project and loved it. I'm sure he'll take on yours. Just ask."

Cee-cee nodded, her smile growing larger. "I will."

"Good, now let's go look at that apartment," Stephanie said.

The two-bedroom apartment was in worse shape than the lower two floors, with ancient appliances, a pink-tiled bathroom, and more peeling wallpaper, but the views out the back were even more stunning than the ones below.

"I love it," Cee-cee said quietly as she stared out the grimy window.

"What about Tilly? There are a lot of stairs which might become problematic. Cocker spaniels tend to have back issues when they get older."

"She's still young and who knows where I'll be living in five years. I'm more concerned with taking her outside to do her business, but there's some grass out back." Cee-cee took in a deep breath, then let it out, beaming. "I want it."

"Are you sure, Cee-cee?" While Stephanie could see the potential, she was surprised Cee-cee wasn't daunted by the sheer amount of elbow grease that would be needed to make this place shine. Heck, it was daunting to Stephanie, and it wasn't even her project.

"I'm sure," Cee-cee said, her shoulders squared with determination. "I'm going to make this work."

Based on the glow in Cee-cee's eyes, Stephanie had no doubt it was true.

Chapter Fourteen

C elia pressed a hand to her stiff lower back and gazed around the room with a smile. She'd signed her new lease a week ago, and so far, so good. Granted, it was slow going. Like, molasses slow, but she was having *fun*. Each new improvement she made felt like an accomplishment, even if it was just the washing of the windows, or a coat of paint. She'd gotten super lucky with the appliances—two of the three ovens only needed some maintenance, and the rest of the appliances were shipshape and just needed a good cleaning.

Her mind instantly shot to the upstairs apartment that she still hadn't started on. The thought of all the renovation it needed made her wince. Fortunately, she had another week left before she had to vacate the beach house. Now that she and her sisters had finally worked out a more equitable schedule for looking after Pop, she'd managed to use that free time to box most of the stuff she was taking and prep for the move. At this rate, though, it looked like she'd have to live in the apartment while she worked on it. The shop had to be the priority if she wanted to take full advantage of what was left of the summer tourist season. Winters in

Bluebird Bay were long and cold, and while she hoped to get some good business going with the locals during the off-season, the income from August alone could make a huge difference to her bottom line for her first year.

A sharp rap on the door pulled her from her thoughts and she set down the wallpaper scraper she'd been holding to answer it.

"Hey!" she said with a grin as she opened the door to find Mick standing there with what looked like an aloe plant in one hand and a toolbox in the other. His hair was damp and she got a waft of Irish Spring soap as he stepped inside.

"Already started drizzling out there. I think it's going to be a real doozy," he said, giving her an approving once over. "I like this look. It says 'Stay out of my way, I'm renovating…but I'm also a really good baker.'"

She looked down at her apron emblazoned with the image of a latte and the phrase, 'Not until I've had my coffee.' "This one was all stained anyway, so I figured I might as well get paint on it instead of getting it on my clothes. You can see how well that's going," she chuckled, pointing to the cherry red splotch on her cotton T-shirt.

"Great color, though," Mick said, his gray-blue eyes sparkling.

"Yeah, I'm using it for the accent wall in the back."

When Steph had suggested hiring Mick to work on the place, Celia had almost chickened out on asking him. Part of her worried he'd be a distraction, but there was little sense in missing out on the best carpenter in town just because she'd had a crush on him thirty years before.

As he set down his toolbox, biceps flexing beneath his short-sleeve shirt, she found her pulse beating a little faster.

So maybe she hadn't *totally* gotten over her attraction to him. That didn't mean they couldn't work well together. If she got to enjoy the view while they did, all the better.

Satisfied with her very mature and evolved decision, she swiped her hands down her apron.

"I've got this gummy stuff all over my fingers from trying to get the wallpaper in the bathroom down. Why don't I go wash it off, grab you a cup of Joe, and I can show you where I'd like you to start?"

"Sure thing. First, though, I brought you this." He handed the tiny aloe plant over with a smile. "It's sort of a Rafferty tradition. My great-grandmother has the original plant, and she passed pieces of it down to all of her kids. Mine is now the size of a kitchen table, and I give pieces to friends whenever they move into a new place."

Her skin flushed at the sweet gesture, but she told herself that he'd likely given out hundreds of pieces. "This is fabulous, Mick, thank you!"

He toed the floor with his scuffed workbook, looking slightly embarrassed. "They aren't much to look at, but they are really miracle plants. If you get a burn while you're baking, break off a little piece and rub it on your wound. It works wonders."

"My Nana used to have one. I don't know what happened to it after she passed, but I remember she used to put it on our bee stings, scrapes, and sun burns. What a thoughtful gift, Mick."

She found herself blinking back a sudden rush of tears, which was ridiculous, but this little plant was the most thoughtful present anyone had gotten her for as long as she could remember. Certainly nothing like the vacuum cleaner and gym membership Nate had gotten her for their anniversary.

"No problem," Mick said.

They stared at one another for a long moment until she cleared her throat. "Anyway, let me wash my hands and get you that coffee. Feel free to take a look around, make some notes, check the place out."

She scurried toward the door leading downstairs to the kitchen, feeling like a seventeen-year-old girl again. By the time she walked back up with mugs in hand, she had gotten control over her emotions and was ready to get down to business. This place was her own personal elephant and the only way to eat it was one bite at a time.

"Thanks," Mick said, taking the mug from her with a nod. "You were right. This space is a steal. Lots of cosmetic stuff, but the bones are good and that view…"

They both looked out the now-clean windows and sighed, almost in stereo, which caused them to break out into laughter.

"I'm a sucker for the ocean. Especially when it's like this," he said. The sky was overcast and gray as rain pelted the glass, but the water was stunning. A riot of blues and greens, with waves crashing onto the craggy coast. "A bunch of family friends moved south as they got older, and they always asked my parents why they stayed here." He gestured to the sight before them and shrugged. "This is why. It's a part of me."

"Me too," Cee-cee agreed, taking a sip from her steaming cup. "That's why I've decided not to go super cutesy or youthful with the interior. Rather than painting cupcakes or sweets on the wall, I'm going to make the view the star." She pointed to the space in front of her. "I want six little espresso tables here, almost like a French patisserie, so people feel invited to stay and eat their cake with a nice cappuccino or cup of tea. And then over there"—she gestured to the front of the store—"I want to set up two, small cylindrical cases with cupcake towers on display, specifically geared toward weddings and other high-end events. Of course, there will be another long case in front with the counter and register, and then, last but not least, I want to have a little space carved off with a half-wall. Inside, there'll be a massive table and tiny chairs. I was thinking that families with kids could come in for cupcake-decorating classes every Saturday. We'd really deck that part of the shop out and go full Wonka in there because it's for children and they love that stuff. I just know my own kids would've been ecstatic if I took them to a place like that when they were young."

She knew she was babbling, but she couldn't seem to stop herself. She was just so excited. Already, she could visualize every single detail in her mind. If she was this crazy now, she wondered if she might explode once it was actually done.

"Is it too much?" she asked, a sudden blast of fear and uncertainty blowing over her like a frigid, winter breeze.

She turned to find Mick staring at her, a bemused smile of wonder tipping his firm lips.

"Nope. It's just right."

For one, long beat, the space around them seemed to shrink, and Cee-cee forgot all about cupcakes. Then Mick cleared his throat and shook his head a little as if to clear it, breaking the spell.

"I mean, so long as your new landlord is okay with structural additions?"

"She's okay with just about anything I do, to be honest. She's ecstatic a woman business owner is taking over the space and has offered to kick in ten thousand to do renovations in the apartment to help increase the value of the property. She's given me carte blanche as long as I'm willing to foot the bill for everything above the ten grand. I just had to sign an agreement I'd paint the place white if and when I leave, which won't be a problem, because I'm not leaving."

She felt a rush of self-consciousness again and chuckled a little at herself. "That probably sounds overly optimistic to you. I know that most businesses fail in the first year, but—"

"Stop it, Cee-cee," Mick's gravelly voice cut in.

She paused and swallowed hard. "Stop what?"

"Stop putting yourself down. Your ideas for this place are great. You're an amazing baker. You *should* feel confident it's going to succeed. Remember in high school, how you decided to run for student council senior year because the food in the cafeteria was so bad?"

She nodded, feeling her cheeks flush. "I remember. I'm surprised you do, though."

"Well, it was a pretty impressive feat. First time running and you beat out the sitting president and the entire cabinet," he said with a chuckle. "By November, our lunches had gotten a serious upgrade. That's the Cee-cee I know. And it's great to see her again. Don't try to hide her away…she's pretty great."

"Thanks, Mick," Cee-cee murmured. She took a sip from her quickly cooling coffee because she couldn't figure out what else to do with her hands. Mostly, she wanted to wrap them around Mick and squeeze, because he'd said the exact right thing at the exact right moment. She was very lucky to have him in her corner on this project.

Speaking of which, this work wasn't going to do itself…

"Okay, let's dig in and get started."

The rest of the day went by in a whirlwind of activity. Mick was a machine, blasting through task after task with no signs of flagging energy. By the time evening rolled around, he'd put up the studs for the half-wall she'd requested and started repairing the dumbwaiter. She'd gotten a fair bit done herself, finishing the wallpaper job, then started getting the downstairs kitchen in order, and even baking a test batch of cupcakes to make sure the oven temperatures were properly calibrated.

It was almost six o'clock when she and Mick stood on separate floors of the shop, talking to each other on their cell phones.

"Okay, ready to test 'er out?" Mick asked. She could hear the smile in his voice and couldn't help but smile back.

"Ready!"

She closed the door of the now-clean and hopefully functioning dumbwaiter. When they'd tried it earlier, the rope had been so old and frayed, it had broken. Mick had installed a sturdy wire instead, and they were about to give it a trial run. Little did he know, she was putting her full trust in his skills because she'd stuck an entire tray of cupcakes in the box before giving him the go-ahead. As the pulley began to move, she held her breath.

"Seems like it's working," Mick said.

"Yesss!" she said, pumping her fist.

"Yup, here it is now. Wow, you really rolled the dice on that one, didn't you?" Mick said with a chuckle. "These look delicious. What flavor?"

"Those are called creamsicle. Blood orange and honey vanilla bean. I, um, remembered back in high school when the ice cream man would come to the lake, you always used to get creamsicles, so it was meant to be sort of a thank you for everything you're doing..." She trailed off, suddenly embarrassed by the silly gesture.

High school was thirty years ago. What had she been thinking? He probably no more liked creamsicles than he did Bob Seger or the blueberry wine they'd used to sneak from his dad's stash to drink at bonfires.

"Mick?" she asked, even more mortified by his sudden and total silence.

"Shhh," he mumbled, his mouth clearly full of cake. "Don't wake me up because I think I'm dreaming."

Relief flooded her, leaving her almost dizzy with it. "Oh, good! I was thinking maybe you didn't like those flavors anymore."

"I don't like them. I love them. This is legitimately the best thing I've ever eaten. You're a genius, Cee-cee."

She reached one hand behind her and patted herself on the back, grinning from ear to ear.

"That's what I want to hear. Okay, save me one, I'll be right up!"

She took a second to wash her hands and then took a quick glance at her reflection on the oven door. As she'd suspected, she was a hot mess. But then she took a closer look and saw something different. Her cheeks were pink with joy and she was practically glowing.

This was it. This was her happy place. Her happy *life*. Giving people joy through food wasn't just her passion...it was her calling. Her only regret was that it had taken her so long to realize it.

She turned away and mounted the stairs with more energy than she deserved to have, given the rigors of the day. When she reached the top, she found Mick standing in front of the windows, staring at the ocean, a fresh cupcake in hand.

"The first one was good, but I wanted to make sure they were all baked consistently, so..."

"It's the only responsible thing to do." She nodded solemnly and followed his gaze, still mesmerized by the scene before her. The drizzle had turned to a full-on downpour, and the ocean was a writhing mass of power and untamed beauty.

Just as she was admiring the wildness of it all, a bright flash flickered in the sky and a loud crack followed. A second later, they were plunged into darkness, with only the haziest light from the moon illuminating the room.

"Uh, Mick?" Cee-cee said.

"Yeah, wow. That was a doozy. Probably going to be a bit before we get power back. Storm's still raging."

She squinted and leaned closer as her eyes adjusted. "Are you just calmly eating that cupcake right now?"

She could barely make out the outline of his broad shoulders shrugging. "If not eating it would make the lights go back on, I'd stop, but..."

She could hear the laughter in his voice and couldn't help but grin. "Fine. I'll join you, then. But let's make a note to look into the cost of a generator. I have butter and all sort of cold items already stocked in the fridge and I'd hate to lose it all."

"Roger that, boss," he replied, happily munching away as she carefully made her way to the dumbwaiter. "I have a six pack of beer in my truck," Mick added. "If you want to have a little picnic while we wait to see if the power comes back. If it's not restored by the time we finish, I can grab a cooler from my place for the perishables."

"This isn't your problem, Mick. Don't feel like you have to stay. I can go home and just come back in a couple hours to check on it."

"Not going to happen," he replied, passing her as he headed for the door. "Looks like the whole block is out," he observed, before stepping out into the storm on a gust of wind.

The word "gentleman" didn't even begin to describe Mick Rafferty, she mused as she bustled around the dim space to find the box where she'd stowed her linens. When she found it, she selected a white tablecloth and spread it out on the floor.

Mick came back in a minute later with a tiny lantern and a six-pack in hand. "I forgot I had this in my emergency roadside kit. Should come in handy."

For the next hour, the two of them sat on the floor drinking lukewarm beer and eating cupcakes. But mostly, they talked. About his parents and his brother, Joe. About his work and how much he loved creating things with his hands. Even about her and Nate. Mick had made it clear that he was going to do his best to be cordial on the topic of her ex, but every so often, she would catch an eyeroll or flash of anger by the light of his little lantern that made her want to hug him.

"Look, I'm not going to say I'm a fan of the guy. And what he did was…" Mick trailed off and Cee-cee could see he was choosing his words very carefully. "Let's just say that's not something I can respect, as a man. But at the end of the day, even if he handled it like a coward, he did you a favor, Cee-cee. If he had stayed, you'd have probably taken years to work up the courage to leave him."

She appreciated that Mick gave her that much credit. She was pretty sure Cee-cee 1.0 would've died in that house, tethered to that man in an unfulfilling marriage, but she didn't correct him.

"I agree. It took a little while for me to see it, but now it's so clear. I'm in such a better place, mentally and emotionally. If only I could apply all this good fortune to the situation with my dad, everything would be right with the world."

Mick kicked out his long legs and leaned back on his hands as he regarded her. "I heard what happened a little while back with your dad walking home in the rain and all. Not doing so well?"

Cee-cee took a swig of her beer and shrugged. "I see people in their late seventies and early eighties who are totally immobile or unable to see, and sometimes I think he's doing great. But the mental stuff...it's hard to watch. I think I handle it the best of the three of us. Anna manages him okay when she's in town, but her brain is off in Portugal or Honduras half the time, even when she's here. Right now, she's in the middle of a shoot at this puffin sanctuary about an hour or so out of town, and she's still not fully present. She'll forget it's her night to take care of dad and call last minute to tell me she's going to be late. And Steph has her own issues with Pop that I don't think she's really worked through..."

Cee-cee trailed off, already feeling guilty for talking about her sisters in a negative way.

"I love them both dearly and I understand we can't all have the same strengths," she added quickly. "I'm just at a time in my life where I have to be a bit selfish with my time if I want to get this business off the ground, move out of the beach house, and get into my new apartment."

"That's not selfish, Cee-cee. That's just not self-*less*. There's a difference," Mick said softly.

She took a moment to mull his statement over. He was right. "Anyway, I'm blessed beyond measure. My kids are doing okay. Max's bookstore is off to a slow start, but she has a bunch of promotional events planned, so I'm hopeful she'll succeed. Plus, she already found a roommate and moved out of the house. I was worried about Gabe and Sasha, but they're trying to work things out. They're taking it slow, but I feel like they're meant to be."

"And if they aren't, that's okay, too," Mick said, his gaze thoughtful. "You know it's not your job to make sure everyone is happy, right, Cee-cee? All you can control is you. Let your sisters know what you can commit to for your father's care, and if they can't pull their weight, the three of you can hire a part-time nurse or aide to help with the rest. Don't waste time or energy on resentment or wishing you could change someone else. I know your life is going well right now, but I think you'd be even more fulfilled if your own happiness wasn't dependent on every single person you love being perfectly content, as well. That's just not how life works."

When he said it like that, it seemed so obvious, but it really was a revelation. A kick in the head by a mule kind of epiphany.

"Amen to all of that. Not just a master carpenter, but also one heck of a life coach." She held up her beer bottle and tipped it in Mick's direction, mind reeling. "Here's to letting go of other people's crap and focusing on my own."

He clinked his bottle to hers and smiled. "To letting go."

Chapter Fifteen

W hy are we doing this again?" Anna grunted while she arched back on her knees, trying to reach for her ankles. "Do I *look* like a llama?"

Celia broke into laughter and fell onto her side on her yoga mat. "It's *camel* pose."

"Llama. Camel. What's the difference?" Anna flopped onto her back, staring up at the ceiling. "It should be named pretzel pose. It's more accurate."

"And it's good for you," Stephanie said, speaking in an undertone as she mimicked the instructor's flawless form. "It strengthens your back and your core."

"All it's doing is making my back spasm." Anna continued to lay on the floor, waiting for the cramp to ease. "And it figures you'd be good at it. You're good at everything."

"Get into child's pose," Stephanie said. "It will stretch out your back."

"I don't feel like sticking my butt up in the air right now," Anna grunted.

Cee-cee's giggles renewed. "That's downward dog. This is child's pose." Still on her knees, she folded herself forward, stretching out her arms.

"That should be named 'bow before your leader pose'," Anna said, trying to get back up onto her knees.

"Shh!" the yoga instructor whisper-shouted from the front of the room.

Anna shot her a death stare—so far the only okay part of this class was that they were at the back and could get away with a little talking—but the spritely young woman had already returned to gazing up at the ceiling. After a moment, she looked up at the class again, giving them a zen smile. "Okay, ladies, let's transition to warrior pose."

"Warrior?" Stephanie whispered to her sisters. "We need to stretch out our backs. That's not a natural flow."

"I say we give this up and go eat cupcakes," Anna said, now sitting with her legs out in front of her.

Stephanie frowned, and Anna was sure her older sister was irritated with her, but then Stephanie stretched into her own child's pose, ignoring the instructor's directive.

"Is there a problem back there, ladies?" the instructor called out, now in warrior pose.

"There will be if someone gets injured," Stephanie said, her voice muffled by the mat in her face. "We need to do a counter stretch after that pose."

"Oh...I understand," the younger girl said with a dismissive nod, then told the class, "Now switch sides."

The teacher's condescending tone set Anna off. "What *exactly* do you understand?"

The twenty-something woman grimaced and said, "You know...older bodies."

"*Older* bodies?" Anna asked, getting to her feet. "How old do you think I am?"

The instructor's grimace widened, showing teeth. "Old enough for *retirement?*" her voice rose at the end, making it sound like she was guessing.

Anna gaped. "*Retirement?* I'm only forty-eight."

Cee-cee started giggling again.

The younger woman's face reddened in embarrassment. "Perhaps you three should leave. It's obvious this isn't the right yoga class for you."

"It's a beginner's class," Anna protested.

"There are some geriatric online videos," the instructor suggested. "Those might be more up your alley."

Several women in the class looked embarrassed, but a few stared in rapt attention.

"What?" Anna asked. "That's ageism."

Stephanie, who'd already gotten to her feet, grabbed her arm. "Anna, I think we should just leave."

"She insulted me," Anna said in disbelief, turning back to look at her. "Shoot, she insulted you and Cee-cee, too, since you're both older than *me!*"

Stephanie leaned closer. "I know, but let's just go. We clearly aren't welcome here." She squatted and picked up her mat, still unrolled, and carried it out of the studio.

Grumbling, Anna did the same, trailing her sister into the fitness studio hall, waiting for the still-laughing Cee-cee to join them.

"I can't believe you let her get away with that!" Anna said to her sisters, tossing her mat onto the floor. She turned to Stephanie. "And *you* just walked out."

Stephanie gave her an ornery grin, then squatted and started to roll up her mat. "Choose your battles, little sister."

Anna filled with mischievousness. "Does that mean you're going to put firecrackers in her shoes like you did to

Maryanne Carpenter back in high school after she dropped you in the cheerleading pyramid at the homecoming game?"

Stephanie shook her head, suppressing a grin. "*You* put a firecracker in her shoe, and no. I have something better in mind." Her mat now rolled, she straightened.

"You can't get much better than a firecracker in a shoe," Anna grumbled.

Cee-cee stared at them in disbelief. "When on earth did that happen?"

"You'd already left for college," Stephanie said. "Anna and Maryanne didn't see eye to eye."

"You were the cheerleading captain and she wanted your spot," Anna insisted, dropping to the floor to roll her own mat. "And why did we think yoga was a good idea?"

Stephanie had been doing yoga at home for years after studying with a yogi while in college. She'd tried to get her sisters to try it with her, but they'd always turned her down. Until now. Cee-cee had agreed because she'd decided she'd wasted too many years *not* trying things, and Anna...she'd only agreed because she wanted to fix her relationship with Stephanie. And if yoga was what it took, she'd grin and bear it...then get out the ibuprofen and a heating pad later. Besides, she needed to get on Stephanie's good side before she brought up a subject that was sure to disrupt their tentative truce.

"It's good for stretching out muscles and improving posture," Stephanie said, waiting on her sisters. "With Cee-cee and all her renovation and you squatting and climbing on rocks to take photos of those tiny, fluffball birds, I figured you could use a good yoga class. Little did I know it would be taught by a child who's encouraging unsafe practices." She started to walk down the hall, then turned back to point her finger at her sisters. "That was supposed to be a beginner class. No one flows from camel to warrior. She's not teaching true beginners the proper foundations. They'll need to relearn everything... that is, if they don't injure themselves. It's a liability to the studio." She spun around and stomped toward the front door.

"Is she leaving us here?" Cee-cee asked, sounding half worried and half proud.

"I don't know," Anna said, staring at Stephanie as she rounded a corner with determination in her eyes. "But I haven't see her this worked up in years."

"Not since before Paul died," Cee-cee said.

Anna frowned. She was right. "Let's go catch her before she takes off without us."

They finished rolling up their mats and headed for the exit. But when they turned the corner, Anna was surprised to see Stephanie hadn't left after all. She was in a huddle with the fitness center manager outside the woman's office. Stephanie finished whatever she'd been saying about the instructor's unsafe practices and the manager said something Anna couldn't hear.

Stephanie's eyes widened. "Oh, no... I couldn't possibly do that."

"Just consider it," the manager said. "We can discuss hours and pay later." With that, she shook Stephanie's hand and headed back to her office.

"Did the manager just offer you a job?" Cee-cee asked, incredulous.

"I think so," Stephanie said, still in shock. Then she seemed to snap out of it. "Let's go." She took off down the hall again, moving much too fast for someone who'd been in that class.

"How did *that* happen?" Anna asked, trying to catch up. Her back was still cramping on her left side.

"Well…" Stephanie said, digging her car keys out of her bag as they left the building. "I told her about my background with yoga and why I was concerned with Katie's instructions. The next thing I knew, she was asking me to teach a beginners' class twice a week."

"That's amazing!" Cee-cee said, clapping her hands together.

"It's ridiculous," Stephanie said. "I've never taught a yoga class before."

"That's not true," Cee-cee said. "You taught at Sarah's high school. Remember? They had a yoga club and Sarah signed you up."

"Those were a bunch of high school girls nearly ten years ago. That does *not* make me a yoga teacher."

"It might be good for you," Anna said. "Get you out of the house and the office, interacting with people."

"I see people," Stephanie said as she yanked her car door open. "I see pet owners all day long."

"I think what Anna's trying to say," Cee-cee said carefully as she climbed into the backseat, "is that a change of pace might be nice."

"I like my life the way it is," Stephanie said. "I have a routine. It's bad enough that I have two nights taken up with Pop." Horror filled her eyes as soon as the words left her mouth. "I didn't mean it like that."

But Anna was certain she had.

They were quiet as Stephanie drove them to Mo's, and Anna was starting to regret that she'd suggested they do dinner after yoga. Her truce with Stephanie was tentative at best, and her sister was obviously on edge. It didn't help that Anna was about to bring up a topic guaranteed to piss her off.

"Well, I thought trying a yoga class was nice," Cee-cee said. "Even if Anna threw out her back with the pretzel pose."

All three women laughed and some of the tension eased.

They were chatting again by the time they got to the diner and took their seats, discussing Cee-cee's progress on the shop, Anna's puffin shoot, and the rehabilitation of Stephanie's rescue turtle. It felt like old times, or at least the times that Anna had shared with her sisters. There was no denying Cee-cee and Stephanie had a closer relationship than Anna had with either of them, and she knew her career was to blame for keeping her away. Which made what she had to say all the harder.

She waited until they'd ordered and gotten their food to drop the bomb.

"I was offered a new assignment."

Stephanie and Cee-cee froze, both likely knowing what was coming next.

"I thought the puffins were keeping you busy for at least another month," Cee-cee said, her forehead wrinkled with confusion.

"They are…" Anna said. "But some of the early photos have caught the eye of a foundation that works to protect polar bears. They've asked me to come photograph polar bears in the wild for their website and fundraising."

Both women stared at her until Stephanie put down her fork. "When?"

"Next month. Five weeks from now, so we have some time—"

"And how long would you be gone?" Stephanie cut in, her tone icy.

"I'm not sure," Anna said with a shrug. "It depends on how hard they are to find, what kind of shots I get..." Her voice trailed off.

"How long?" Stephanie asked, sounding sterner. "Ball park."

Anna tried not to cringe when she said, "Three months. Maybe four."

Cee-cee's mouth opened as she started to say something then stopped to think it over. Finally, she said, "I see."

"I can tell them no," Anna said.

Stephanie's eyes pierced hers. "So tell them no."

"But it's the chance of a *lifetime*," Anna said. "I've been invited to shoot in the Arctic National Park. They don't just let anyone have access."

Her sisters remained silent.

"I'll tell them no," she said, although her wrists itched under imaginary shackles.

Stephanie's face twisted. "I find it so ironic that you've given me a lecture about stepping up and helping more with Pop, yet the first chance you get to leave, you're up and off without a second thought about the responsibilities you'll be leaving behind."

"Trust me when I tell you this isn't the first chance I've had to leave. I've passed up multiple offers in order to stay and help Cee-cee with the transition after Nate. But, counter to what little Miss Katie might think, I'm not retired yet. This is my *job*, Stephanie," Anna said with a bit more force than necessary. "I've been doing it for years, and I've stayed home longer than I usually do. I don't know why this comes as a surprise."

"Maybe," Stephanie said, leaning closer, "it's because I thought you were ready to finally accept responsibility, but it turns out I'm wrong."

"I've accepted responsibility," Anna protested, irritation and guilt meddling together into a ball of hot anger. "But does it mean I need to give up my life and my entire career to stay and help take care of Pop?"

"You insisted that I do my part," Stephanie countered, not giving an inch. "You need to do yours, too."

"I can't help it if my job takes me out of town," Anna said.

"What about your puffin job?" Stephanie asked. "Get more jobs like that."

"I would if I could, but—"

"That's crap, Anna, and you know it," Stephanie said, grabbing her purse. "You're only responsible when it's convenient for you. It's no longer convenient, so off you go."

"It's different for you and Cee-cee," Anna objected. "You're both here. Your kids are gone…"

"Right. I've got nothing but my job, same as you," Stephanie said in a cold tone. "My career is my life and I still make it work with Pop on my scheduled days."

"*Now* you do," Anna shot back. "After we called you on the fact that you never went to see him."

"Please don't fight," Cee-cee cut in, watching them in dismay. "I hate it when you fight."

"Don't worry," Stephanie said as she slid out of the booth. "She won't be here much longer to fight with."

"Where are you going, Steph?" Anna asked, irritation creeping into her voice. "You can't just leave us here."

"That would be the irresponsible thing to do, wouldn't it?" Stephanie asked. "I guess I have a month or so of my own irresponsibility left before you run off with yours." She walked out of the diner without a backward glance.

Anna turned to her stunned sister.

"You're really going to take the job?" Cee-cee asked, her eyes glassy.

How did Anna explain this to her sister to help her understand? "I've tried to stay, Cee-cee, honestly, I have, and the puffin job has kept me happy, but the truth is that wildlife photography is in my blood. It's who I am." She reached across the table and snagged her sister's hand. "Asking me to give it up would be like asking Stephanie to give up healing pets. Or asking you to give up baking again. Those things define us. They're part of who we are." She paused, worried she'd sound melodramatic. "If I give it up, I'll go crazy, Cee-cee. And this isn't just any job. This is a once-in-a-lifetime opportunity. I'll never forgive myself if I pass it up."

Cee-cee squeezed Anna's hand. "Then you need to go."

"But Stephanie…"

She squeezed again. "I'll deal with Stephanie."

"Cee-cee—"

"Don't you worry about it," Cee-cee said with a tight smile and tears in her eyes. "This is your decision to make. Not mine and not Stephanie's. Trust me, it's taken me years to accept that I need to make myself happy before I can ever make anyone else happy."

"*Are* you happy, Cee-cee?"

Cee-cee smiled. "Yeah, I actually am." She leaned closer. "And I want you to be happy, too. If that means going to photograph polar bears… I think you're insane, but you need to go." She winked. "I thought you were insane long before you started photographing polar bears."

Anna laughed despite the tears in her eyes.

"Life's too short to be miserable," Cee-cee said, her tone insistent. "Once we get a little closer to the date you leave, we can discuss hiring a part-time person to fill in the gaps or something. You need to follow your heart."

"But what if my heart wants both? To be here and to go?"

Cee-cee's smile turned sad. "I don't know, but I know you'll pick what's right for you, and I'll be cheering you all the way." She swallowed and her voice cracked. "I love you, Anna. Be happy."

Anna wanted to be happy, but no matter which path she picked, she knew there would be heartache.

Chapter Sixteen

Celia lay back in the bath with a sigh of bliss.

Done.

She almost laughed out loud at the thought. Not *done-done*, but she'd managed to clean out the rest of the beach house, move her stuff into the new apartment, get Tilly acclimated, and even get the essentials unpacked, which was saying something. Better yet? She and Nate were done.

Done-done. They'd made it official the day before at the courthouse. She'd half expected to be an emotional basket case afterward. Not because she still loved Nate—since he'd left, she'd realized it had been a long time since she'd loved him the way a person should love their spouse—but just because it was the end of an era. Anna had told her about her shorthand for Celia's life before Nate: B.N. Well, the divorce meant she'd officially moved on to the period of her life that was P.N. *Post* Nate.

Tears for what they'd lost would've been completely understandable. Normal, even. But there had been none. Just a bittersweet moment that had passed between them as they looked at each other from opposing tables.

She'd walked out into the sunshine, alone in spite of her sisters' request to come for support, and wanted to click her heels together in jubilation. The only single ounce of sadness hadn't come from the money she could've gotten, or because she'd lost the house. It was for the man she'd thought Nate had been. That person, she mourned.

Not for long, though. His cheating butt and Amanda Meadows were made for each other, and he could sleep in the bed he'd made on that front. Celia, for one, was a happier person today than she'd been a few months ago. She wondered idly if she should thank him for leaving.

"Nah, screw that."

Celia shifted in the steamy water with a chuckle, letting her eyes drift shut as she considered the evening ahead. Freedom-fest had been Anna's idea, naturally. At first, Celia had refused, but her youngest sister was nothing if not convincing. To Celia's relief, Stephanie had agreed to come, as well, hopefully signaling the end to what Celia and Max had been secretly referring to as The Big Chill for the past week since Anna and Steph's blowout after yoga class.

Not that her sisters were actively fighting. Actually, that might've been better. No, instead they steered around each other like two ships passing, with one honking a fog-horn at the other every so often just to be ornery. If either one of them tried to pull that crap tonight, she planned to shut it down. Once Anna had sold her on the idea of going out tonight, Cee-cee was all about it. She'd picked up an amazing, butter-yellow sundress for the occasion. It left her tanned shoulders bare and made her feel pretty, and super daring to boot.

She wondered idly if they'd run into Mick while they were out. She opened her eyes, sloshing water around as she sat up to reach for the tray that lay across the tub. On it sat a creamsicle cupcake and an icy glass of lemonade. Ever since she'd made them for Mick a few weeks back, they'd become her go-to cake with the tart bite of the blood orange tempered by the smooth, woody flavor of vanilla.

Mick's favorite cupcake wasn't the only thing she'd taken a liking to—she'd enjoyed the six pack they'd shared that night. They'd shared a couple more since then and she had to count herself as a convert. Wouldn't Nate be horrified to know that she'd dumped Pinot Grigio for Dos Equis?

She grinned as she bit into the moist cake with a sigh. She and Mick had made a great team on the remodel and she'd miss having him underfoot. He'd been so great with everything. He'd even helped her move into the apartment. It had been on the tip of her tongue to invite him along for tonight's festivities, but she'd stopped herself. It was probably better for it to be just the girls—Cee-cee, her friend Jackie who was in town for the week visiting her parents, Steph, and Anna. Not to mention the gossip it would cause if she brought a man along with her to her divorce celebration. Tongues would already be wagging, and throwing Mick into the mix would just make it worse. Still, it was going to be weird not seeing him all the time.

The phone she'd laid on the tray buzzed, distracting her from her thoughts, and she picked it up, noting Anna's name across the screen.

"Hey, sis."

"We're outside and the door is locked. Let us in, or we'll start Freedom-fest without you right here on the sidewalk!"

The fiendish joy in Anna's voice filled her with excitement mixed with a healthy dose of fear, but she recovered quickly. "Give me two minutes," Celia said before disconnecting.

She set the tray onto the floor and climbed out of the tub, taking a quick second to wrap her hair in a towel. After pulling on her favorite fluffy robe, she hustled down the back staircase, Tilly hot on her heels. A bug-eyed Anna already had her face pressed to the glass of the floor-to-ceiling window by the front door.

"Woohoo, she's already half-naked and ready for action!" she whooped, just barely audible through the wood and glass.

Celia bit back a laugh and let the three grinning women in, throwing her arms around Jackie with a squeal.

"I'm so glad you're here for this!"

Jackie hugged her back tightly. "I wouldn't miss it for the world. I'd wanted to come when Nate first left, but I'd already taken time off for our spa weekend and then Anthony winding up in the hospital and all..." Her friend pulled away, expression full of regret.

"Nope, don't you dare apologize. Family first, and regardless, you're here now," Celia replied. "Now let's get back upstairs before I get arrested for flashing the goodies to some poor passerby, shall we?"

"Ha!" Anna snorted as she followed them down the hall and up the stairs. "They should be so lucky."

Steph scooped up Tilly and joined the parade.

The next hour was a whirlwind. Stephanie made a batch of her signature mojitos while Anna and Jackie primped Celia to within an inch of her life. Hair, makeup, the whole deal. Luckily, they all approved of her dress, oohing and ahhing over how the color gave her skin a golden glow and made her eyes pop.

When she looked in the mirror, she let out a small gasp. Her hair fell in a dark tumble around her shoulders, and the artfully applied bronze-y palette made her face look sun-kissed but not made up. She looked like herself, only well-rested and five years younger.

"You guys missed your calling," she said with a whistle. "Ever think of quitting your day jobs?"

It wasn't until she noted Anna's face dim and Steph turn away that she realized she'd touched a nerve.

So much for ending The Big Chill...

"I just meant you could open a salon and—"

"Jackie would be in charge of hair, because she's the one who managed to get those gorgeous waves," Steph said, her tone a little too bright.

"And Steph is always good at picking out the best lipstick color. Angelina Jolie's got nothing on that mouth right now, sis," Anna added with a grin.

It all felt a little forced, but Celia wasn't about to question it. Her sisters had clearly decided not to let their issue rock the boat tonight, and for that, she was thankful.

The foursome finished their cocktails and headed out on foot, taking advantage of the balmy night air.

"Where to first?" Celia asked, anticipation bubbling through her. She was single for the first time in over thirty years. It felt so strange to think that she wasn't half of a couple anymore. Which meant her options were limitless. She could dance with a stranger, or flirt with the waiter, or maybe even share a kiss with someone who wasn't Nate.

"We were thinking dinner at The Lobster Shack and then drinks and karaoke at Benny's Place. Thoughts?" Jackie asked, shooting a glance at Cee-cee as they walked.

"Sounds perfect to me." She was a terrible singer, but she was with her best girls, so what did it matter? Tonight was about having fun.

Dinner was a buttery, delicious mess of lobster and corn on the cob followed by a shared creme brulee that left them all so full, they headed for a stroll along the beach. Once they'd worked off some of the food, laughing and chatting as they went, they headed to Benny's Place.

The sky was at its best, a watercolor painting of pink and orange, so vibrant that Celia stopped just outside the door to admire it for a moment before trailing in behind the others. This was her life now. One full of friendship, sunsets she'd actually take the time to see and appreciate, and a career she knew she was going to love.

The shop would be opening in just over a week, and she couldn't wait.

The bar at Benny's Place was hopping for a Thursday night, and for a minute, she wondered if they'd even get a seat. Then she saw a table with a reserved sign on it that said "Freedom-fest", and she let out a hearty laugh.

"Your throne, Madame," Anna said with a sweep of her hand and a mischievous grin.

Celia took a seat and the others followed suit. A handsome young waiter with a wide smile and dark, curly hair swept into a tidy man-bun came right over and took their drink orders.

"So, which one of you are we celebrating tonight?" he asked, gesturing to the sign with his pen.

"My sister," Steph said, pointing to Celia, "so don't be skimpy on the rum. We'll all take Mojitos, and keep them coming."

Two hours and three Mojitos later, Celia found herself at the mic with her tribe around her and the opening strains of "I Will Survive" by Gloria Gaynor blaring through the speakers.

"At first I was afraid…" they all shout-sung in unison.

The crowd quickly joined in, and soon it was a glass-hoisting, rabble-rousing singalong that had them all breathless from laughter by the time it was over.

When they got back to the table, Celia found their waiter, whose name they'd learned was Taylor, standing beside her seat with a single white rose in his hand.

"For you," he said simply, handing it to her. His gaze was warm and sincere, and she took the flower, cheeks instantly heating.

"That's so sweet. Thank you, Taylor."

The other three women were very busy trying to look like they weren't listening, but their alcohol-impaired efforts failed miserably.

Taylor took a deep breath, his words coming out in a rush. "I know this might seem forward, but you're a beautiful woman and I wondered if you'd like to go out to dinner with me this weekend."

Celia blinked at him, wondering hazily if her sisters had put him up to this. As she peeked furtively out of the corner of her eye, though, the rest of her party looked as stunned as she felt.

This was for real. An adorable, sweet man who could surely be no older than thirty-two was asking her on a date.

"Oh, wow, Taylor. I really appreciate the offer. I'm just not sure…"

He nodded and held up a hand. "If you're worried about the age difference, I just want to say that I'm an old soul and don't have much in common with women my age. But if it's that you're not ready, I totally understand. I wanted to let you know that I find you very attractive, I like your spirit, and I'd love a chance to get to know you better. That's it. The ball is in your court now, and I won't bother you again."

He moved to back away, but she stopped him with a gentle hand on his muscular arm.

"I cannot express with words how good you just made me feel," she said softly, swallowing back the sudden tightness in her throat. "It's been a long time since anyone said anything quite that lovely to me and I will cherish it always. But as evolved as you are on the whole age difference front, I'm afraid I can't say the same for myself. When I look at you, I see a gorgeous guy, with an open heart and a sweet smile...who is almost as young as my son. I'm sorry," she added with a gentle smile.

Further to his credit, Taylor didn't try to act nonchalant or play it off like he'd been kidding. He bent low—geez, what was he, six-two?—and pressed his soft lips to her cheek in the barest of caresses.

"If you ever change your mind, you know where to find me."

He backed away with one last, long glance and disappeared into the crowd.

"Lord have mercy," Jackie crooned, mock fainting against her chair.

Anna picked up a menu and began fanning herself with it furiously. "Are you out of your mind?" she demanded, her eyes wide with disbelief. "That Adonis wanted to take you out and you said no? Did you tell him you had a younger sister who isn't nearly as prissy about dating younger men?"

Even Steph was smiling. "He's a cutie, Cee-cee. I hope you don't regret saying no."

But Cee-cee's thoughts were already somewhere else. Taylor would make whoever was lucky enough to capture his heart a very happy woman, but that woman wasn't her. She replayed his words in her mind and let them marinate for a second.

"If it's that you're not ready..."

Was she ready?

An image floated through her mind and she stood. "Be right back."

Cee-cee made her way out to the back of the bar and stepped onto the patio, where it was quieter. Then, acting on pure adrenaline and instinct, she pulled out her phone. *Don't overthink it. Just do it.*

She punched the screen a few times with a shaking finger and then lifted the phone to her ear, pulse hammering.

"Hello?"

Mick's warm, husky voice washed over her like warm summer rain.

"Mick? It's Cee-cee." She paused and took a deep breath. "Do you want to go on a date with me?"

His reply was instantaneous. "I'm in."

A nervous laugh bubbled from her lips. "I didn't even say where or when!"

"It doesn't matter. Still in," he said, his voice low and husky.

She squeezed her eyes closed and pumped her fist in the air. She and Mick Rafferty were going on a date. If high school Cee-cee could only see her now...

Chapter Seventeen

Celia stared at her reflection in the mirror and smoothed non-existent wrinkles from her new green and ivory, knee-length dress. She'd tried to replicate the look her sisters and Jackie had given her two nights before, and she'd gotten pretty close. Some days, when she stared at her reflection in the mirror of her partially renovated apartment, she couldn't believe she was the same woman she'd been three months ago. *That* woman had tied herself up in bows trying to meet her husband's expectations, but she also had to acknowledge that while Nate had used his persuasion to make her his minion, she had to accept responsibility for letting him.

She shook her head. *No looking back. Only forward.* But she couldn't help reminding herself that Mick was from her past, too, but from a past she remembered with fondness, when she was still Celia, B.N., not Mrs. Nate Burrows. It was a good lesson to never lose herself in someone else's dreams and purpose.

Everyone deserved their own dreams.

After she tucked Tilly into her kennel with her favorite stuffie, she headed downstairs in her ivory wedges, purse in hand, when she heard a knock at the front door of the shop. Mick was waiting on the other side of the glass, holding a bouquet of fresh-cut hydrangeas and wearing a short-sleeved dress shirt, tan pants, and loafers. A smile spread across his face when he saw her and a thousand butterflies took flight in her stomach.

Goodness, wasn't she too old for this? She felt like a teenager again and Mick was here to pick her up for prom.

She unlocked the door and swung it open for him to enter, but he stayed in place, his gaze slowly sweeping down to her toes then back up to her face. "You look beautiful, Cee-cee."

Was she really doing this? Going on a date? At her age? But everything about this man intrigued her, so why not? Even that thirty-something waiter from two nights before had thought she was dateable.

He held out the bouquet of hydrangeas, and she took them, unable to resist the urge to bury her nose into the blooms. "My favorite."

A shy smile stole over his face. "I remembered."

Her gaze lifted slowly, locking with his. Never once in thirty-plus years had Nate bought her a bouquet of her favorite flower, insisting on giving her roses, since they were more expensive and less messy when they dropped their petals.

Her cheeks flushed, and she looked away as she said, "I need to put these in water." When she headed for the stairs, he followed her up to her apartment.

"You've gotten a lot accomplished," he said, glancing around the small living room/kitchen while she grabbed a drinking glass from the cabinet and filled it at the kitchen faucet. She'd left all her crystal vases with Nate.

Releasing a short laugh, she said, "I noticed you didn't say it looks great." She held up her hand, grinning. "Trust me, I know the limitations of this place." She winked. "But it's close to work and you can't beat the view." They both turned to gaze out at the harbor and past it toward the deep blue ocean.

"I can help you fix it up," he said with a soft smile. "I'm not sure if you've heard, but I'm pretty good with that sort of thing."

She laughed again. She loved that he made her feel like a bottle of sparkling water, light and bubbly inside. "I'm sure you could," she said, "but it's a matter of finances at this point. I need to save every penny for the cupcake shop." Slightly embarrassed she couldn't afford to hire him for more work, she focused on unwrapping the paper cradling the flowers and placing them in the tall glass of water.

Tilly made whining noises in her kennel. Mick squatted next to it, opening the door to rub behind her ears. "I wouldn't charge you, Cee-cee," he said, then a playful grin lit up his face. "I've gotten used to having you as an assistant, so it's either hire you to work with me on other jobs, or come work with you on your own place."

Shaking her head with a grin, she said, "You're incorrigible." She nodded to the kennel so he understood she didn't just mean the work, but it warmed her heart to see how much Mick liked her dog. It seemed genuine, not just a ploy to get her to like him.

His face lit up with happiness. "And yet I speak the truth."

Celia propped a hand on her hip. "I'm not letting you work on my apartment for free."

He hesitated as though weighing his words. "It almost feels wrong to have charged you for working downstairs. I enjoyed myself too much."

Her heart skipped a beat and she told herself not to read too much into his statement. He'd also told her that he'd never worked on a cupcake shop before, and they'd had fun collaborating on the layout and design. "Well..." she said carefully. "I'm happy you loved it, but you need to make money. I love making cupcakes, but I plan on charging for them." She gave him a warm smile. "Although I'll still use you as a guinea pig when I'm trying new flavors...if you're willing."

He laughed and patted his enviably flat belly. "I'll find a way to soldier through."

"Come on," she said, shaking her head as she tried to suppress her grin. "I'm starving for something other than cupcakes, and we need to get going if we're going to make our reservation at Bruno's."

He nodded as he closed the kennel and gestured toward the staircase as he stood.

"One thing is certain," she said as her shoes clomped down the stair treads. "My legs are going to be in great shape. It's like my own personal Stairmaster."

He made a sound behind her that sounded like agreement, and he was grinning when they reached the bottom. Apparently, Mick liked what he saw and the realization made her feel like she was floating on air, in spite of the heels.

The restaurant was only a few blocks away, so they decided to walk and enjoy the warm summer evening. They strolled side-by-side, the tourists veering around them on the wide sidewalk. Mick's hand was only inches from hers, which she tried to ignore as they chatted about the town, the weather, and the grand opening of the cupcake shop.

"Everything seems to be coming along like this was meant to be," Mick said.

"True," she said, slightly uneasy. "I keep expecting to wake up and realize this is all a dream. I almost want to pinch myself."

He grabbed her hand and squeezed, flashing her a playful grin. "Thought this might be better than a pinch."

A flutter washed through her as she felt his rough, calloused hand cradle her softer one. Nate had never been a hand holder, and she'd always thought she didn't like it, either, but maybe it had always been the wrong hand.

As they walked up to the entrance of Bruno's, Mick let go and placed his hand at the small of her back, steering her toward the hostess stand.

"Burrows," Celia said as they approached, "party of two."

The hostess glanced at her tablet, then looked up with a smile. "We have a table set up for you. Right this way."

Bruno's was one of the nicer restaurants in Bluebird Bay. The walls were covered in dark wood planks and the decor was reminiscent of the inside of a yacht with lanterns on the walls and rich brocade draperies on the edges of the windows.

She led them to a table overlooking the harbor, an intimate table for two with a small, flickering candle in the middle. When they were seated, Mick fingered the edge of his menu. "I know you asked me out, Cee-cee, but I'd like to pay for dinner."

Celia folded her hands on the crisp white tablecloth. "Nope. This is my treat as a thank you for everything you've done to help me."

He cocked his head. "Then I'll pay for the next dinner as a thank you for all of those cupcakes."

The *next* dinner.

The thought filled her with more happiness than she'd expected. She liked the idea of a next dinner and many more, but she told herself to take this slow. She and Mick were still getting to know each other again, but she couldn't deny that he was basically the same man she'd known years ago, only more mature and confident.

More desirable.

They ordered wine and dinner, then chatted without a single lull in the conversation. "I know you never married," Celia finally said, addressing the elephant in the corner. It had been on her mind and there was such an easy comfort between them now, it only seemed natural to ask. "Is there a reason why?"

He gripped the stem of his wine glass between his thumb and his first two fingers, spinning it slightly on the tablecloth. "I never loved anyone enough to commit to marriage."

"I know you had girlfriends…"

A cocky grin lit up his face. "Were you keeping track of me, Cee-cee?"

She laughed, belying her nervousness at the question. "It's a small town."

He held her gaze, his grin never wavering. "That it is."

"Well?" she pressed.

Still holding her eyes, he said, "I've been waiting for the right woman to come along." She was struck again by his confidence in himself and his choices. It could have come across as arrogance, but there wasn't even a hint of it. She'd noted that about him while they were working together, first on the bookstore and then on her shop. He was very good at what he did, and he knew it, but he never gloated about it. She loved that about him.

Her skin flushed. "Do you feel like you missed out not having a family?"

"One lesson I learned long ago, Cee-cee, was never settle."

Never settle. He was right. She'd spent her life settling, and that was done. She picked up her wine glass and held it up toward him. "To never settling."

He clicked his glass with hers, his gaze roaming her face. "I'll drink to that."

Being with Mick was easy and comfortable, and she wasn't ready for their date to end when the waiter brought them the bill.

Mick was obviously thinking the same thing. "There's a concert in Bluebird Park with fireworks after. Would you like to walk over and check it out?"

Part of her wondered if she should be more coy with him. This was their first date, but she was done playing games and she was done playing it safe. She wasn't going to hide from the wonderful possibilities in her life.

"I would," she said, handing the waiter her credit card. "That sounds lovely."

After she settled the bill and they walked out of the restaurant, Mick snagged her hand again, and her butterflies were back. Friends had dinner together, but this next part definitely made it feel like a date.

The outdoor concert was already in progress when they approached the crowded park, and Celia realized the flaw in their plan. "We don't have a blanket." And as much as she wanted to go, she didn't want to sit on the grass.

Mick grinned. "I planned ahead in case you agreed." He led her to his truck, which he'd parked in the lot for the recreation area.

"You walked all the way from the park to my shop?" she asked. It was nearly a mile.

He shrugged. "It was nothing."

It was far from nothing. He not only had a blanket on the bed of his truck, but also a small picnic basket tucked inside a larger cooler. "What's in there?" she asked, trying to peer inside.

He picked it up, tucking the blanket between his arm and his chest, then snagged her hand again. "You'll see."

They found an empty spot toward the back. Mick spread out the blanket while Celia held the basket, and she was surprised by its weight. He took the basket and gestured for her to sit. When she was settled with her legs tucked to one side, Mick opened the lid and pulled out a bottle of wine, handing her two plastic, stemless wine glasses.

She laughed. "You *did* plan ahead."

"There's more," he said as he started to open the bottle.

"*More?*"

He poured them each a glass of white wine then pulled out a small cardboard box containing four chocolate-covered strawberries.

"You sure do know the way to a woman's heart," she teased.

He clicked his plastic glass against hers. "Let's hope so."

They spent the next hour drinking wine, eating strawberries, and listening to music. Celia couldn't remember the last time she'd enjoyed an evening this much.

When the fireworks started, Mick wrapped his arm around her upper back, helping support her as they stared into the sky. She could smell his familiar scent, fresh and manly, and it surprised her how familiar it already felt.

She glanced back at him, surprised to see he was watching her instead of the show. He smiled and she was sure she would burst with happiness. It had been so long since a man had looked at her like that.

The fireworks ended and they packed up their things and headed to Mick's truck. "Would you like to walk home or drive?" He glanced at the stand-still traffic and laughed. "It might be faster and more enjoyable to walk."

"But you'll have to make the walk twice," she said.

"I don't mind," he said. "It gives me more time to hold your hand."

Her stomach flutters returned as he stashed the basket and took her hand.

They started to walk toward her end of town when Celia heard a familiar voice say, "The ink on your divorce is barely dry, Celia Burrows."

Maryanne Brown.

Mick's hand tightened around Celia's as though to keep her from letting go, but she had no intention of allowing this unhappy woman to stop her from living her life.

"Hello, Maryanne," Celia said in a cordial tone. "Did you enjoy the concert?"

"I heard you were opening a cupcake shop."

Celia smiled, even though she heard a hint of aggression in her tone. "The opening is next week."

"Is that so?"

Pushing out a sigh, Celia said, "I realize that you and my sister Anna have had some issues, but I have nothing against you, Maryanne. Live and let live."

Maryanne just let out a huff as they walked past her. Seeing her had reminded them both about high school, though, and Celia and Mick began reminiscing about football games and parties, and the memorable occasion when the junior class homecoming float had become detached from the truck pulling it and rolled into the harbor.

They both laughed.

"I had a crush on you, you know," he said when they were about a block from her shop.

"I suspected," she said. "Why didn't you ask me out?"

He was silent for a moment. "I knew you wanted to go to college and possibly move away for good. I planned on staying and working with my father, so I suspected we wouldn't work long-term."

She stopped in her tracks and turned to face him. "When did you come to that conclusion?"

"When we were juniors," he said with a frown. "Not long after we were dumped into the ocean on that float."

"But we still had nearly two years before I left for college."

"I liked you, Cee-cee. A lot. I knew a relationship with you wouldn't be a high school crush. I didn't know if I would be able to let you go when it came time for you to head off to college, and I didn't want to be the reason you stayed."

"Mick…" Tears filled her eyes. "That's the most selfless thing anyone has ever done for me."

"Then you need better people in your life."

She reached up onto her tiptoes and placed a gentle kiss on his lips. "I think I'm off to a good start."

He smiled down at her, and they walked to the front door of her shop in their first lull of the evening, but it was far from uncomfortable. Celia couldn't help thinking that they had crossed into new territory, and instead of being scared, she was excited.

Mick waited while she unlocked the door. "I want to see you again, Cee-cee."

She put a hand on her hip and gave him a cocky grin. "Well, I hope so. You promised to spring for dinner next time." Where had this bold Cee-cee come from? Celia realized she'd always been there, sleeping. She'd just needed something to jolt her awake.

He laughed. "A promise is a promise. What are you doing next Tuesday night?"

"Going to dinner with you."

He leaned over and gave her a kiss, soft and full of promise.

Celia felt like her life had been reborn.

Chapter Eighteen

Stephanie tied another silver mylar balloon onto the display case and stood back to admire her handiwork.

"I can't thank you guys enough for coming early and helping me with the last-minute decorations," Cee-cee said, her nerves apparent as she flitted around the room, looking for things to fix.

It was fifteen minutes until the grand opening, and she needn't have worried. The place looked gorgeous. In fact, Steph could barely believe it was the same space they'd looked at a month before. The beautiful display cases were a literal feast for the eyes. Mini-cakes with buttery yellow icing, gooey chocolate ganache, and cheery cherry glazes. Stephanie was already calculating how many she should buy to get her through the week.

But the cakes weren't the only visual punch the new shop delivered. From the elegant yet simple tables and chairs lined up in front of the wall of floor-to-ceiling windows to the view itself, it was a stunner. Bluebird Bay had put on quite the show this morning. The sun shone bright in a periwinkle sky topped off with cotton candy clouds. It was an ideal day for a new beginning, and Steph felt a sizzle of anticipation and excitement for her older sister.

"No problem. I can stay until noon and then come back after a quick neuter job to help you clean up," Steph said with a smile.

Anna nodded. "I'm in for the long haul, too. I've just got to run and make sure Dad has lunch. Other than that, I'm all yours."

Cee-cee shot them both a quick smile of gratitude that only widened when Mick Rafferty stepped into the room.

"Hey, you," Cee-cee said, her cheeks going a pretty pink.

Steph and Anna watched with unabashed curiosity as Mick moved closer. Were they about to make this thing kiss-in-public official?

But Mick leaned down and grazed Cee-cee's cheek with his lips and then pulled away.

"This place looks great and you look even better," he murmured.

Okay, so not quite public, but there was no question that Mick and her sister were working their way up to becoming a bonafide item. They'd had dinner twice last week, two lunch dates since, and Mick was at her place basically every day for at least a couple hours helping her get the apartment in order.

As Celia's sibling, Steph knew she should be worried about her sister jumping into a relationship so soon after her divorce. But Mick wasn't just anyone. He'd been a friend for years and he'd shown more than once that he was dependable and trustworthy. Better yet, he seemed to appreciate Celia for who she was, not who he wanted her to be.

In other words? The anti-Nate.

She knew Cee-cee better than anyone and hadn't seen her more "Cee-cee" in decades. If things worked out between them, no one would be happier than Stephanie. If they didn't, that was fine, too. Between the cupcake shop, her cute little apartment with the amazing view, and having Max back in town, Cee-cee would be just fine without a man.

That thought brought Steph a great swell of contentment on Cee-cee's behalf.

Now if only you could manage the same for yourself...

A knock sounded at the door and Cee-cee smoothed a hand over her apron as she rushed to unlock it. Her grin widened as Max's face appeared in the glass.

"Yay, Mom!" she squealed as the door swung open and she barreled inside. One hand held a riotous bouquet of wildflowers and she used the other to pull her mother into a bear-hug. "Congratulations!"

"Thanks, sweetie, these are gorgeous," Cee-cee said as she accepted the flowers. "I'm so glad you could get away for a little while."

Max's bookstore and Cee-cee's shop were only a few blocks away from each other, but with Max running her place solo and on a shoestring, none of them had been sure if she'd be able to make it.

"I promised Mr. Bonomo a cupcake for him and a second for his son if he'd send him over to mind the bookstore for an hour," Max replied, hefting her purse higher on one shoulder as she winked at her mother. "Moral of that story being, I need you to put aside two of your best creations before they sell out."

Cee-cee chuckled but before she could respond, the bell on the door jingled and Gabe's ex-fiancée, Sasha Posey, stepped in.

Anna shot Stephanie a brow waggle and Steph shrugged in response. Gabe had been trying to reconcile with Sasha. She knew they'd been going to counseling together, but Cee-cee hadn't given her a recent update on where they stood. When the door opened again a moment later and Gabe stepped in to slip an arm around Sasha's waist, she had her answer.

"Hey, Mom," he said, warm affection filling his brown eyes. "Wow, this place looks awesome and smells even better."

"Thanks so much. Mick did such a great job on the renovations, and the rest was a lot of paint and elbow grease. Don't look too closely at anything. I could've used another week, so some of it is holding together with duct tape and a prayer," she added in a stage-whisper.

"Whatever it took, I'm impressed," Sasha said with a tentative smile.

It was clear she was worried that Gabe's family might hold a grudge for their painful if short-lived split, but Cee-cee pulled her into an embrace, which Sasha returned wholeheartedly.

Why can't I be so forgiving? Steph wondered. Even though the worst of her fight with Anna had passed after they'd talked it out before Freedom-fest and vowed to choose their words more carefully, they hadn't hashed out the core of the problem or come up with any solutions. This left a heavy tension between them and she hated it.

So why wasn't she fixing it? Especially with Anna leaving in a few weeks. She'd be in the middle of nowhere in subzero temperatures taking pictures of one of the most deadly creatures on earth. What if, God forbid, she didn't come back?

The thought sent a rush of panic through Steph and she ground her teeth together.

That was ridiculous. Anna was a professional. She'd done countless shoots in equally forbidding locations. Hippos in the Nile, lions of the Serengeti. This was nothing.

But what if it wasn't?

Unbidden, her thoughts shot back to that fateful day two years before. She and Paul were home on a random Wednesday morning. He'd decided to play hookie from work and take the boat out fishing. He'd asked her to join him and she'd declined.

Her last words to him? *"Must be nice getting to fish while I'm spending my day with my fist up a cow's behind."*

Even though she'd said it without any resentment, the memory still haunted her. He'd wanted her to go with him, and she'd brushed aside his invitation like it was nothing. Had she been there, she could've warned him about the incoming storm. She'd have been his first mate, and they could've navigated things together. Instead, he had died alone in the deep, cold waters while she continued to go about her day, clueless.

Worst of all?

She couldn't even remember if she'd said *"I love you"* before he left.

As Mick and Cee-cee led her kids and Sasha around on a tour, Steph stayed behind with Anna, trying to keep her emotions—which were far too close to the surface right now—in check.

"Got all your ducks in a row for the big assignment?" she asked, trying to keep her tone light.

Anna looked understandably wary as she nodded, sending her frizzy curls bobbing. "Pretty much. I have my neighbor Sally coming in to check on the plants, and I think

I've got a great idea for someone who could pinch hit for me on the whole Pop front. I don't want to say too much until I've hammered out the details, but I think it could be a good thing."

Steph leaned back against the countertop, schooling her features to ensure she didn't pull a face. It was hard, because while she wanted to make peace with her little sister, she still couldn't quite understand why she had to leave.

Accept the things you can't change, Stephanie. That's your biggest problem.

Paul used to tell her that all the time, and he was so right. Because of her inability to accept his death, her house had become a veritable shrine to his life, her life a quest to run faster than the memories of her old life chasing her.

She wasn't going to let her issues drive a deeper wedge between her and Anna.

"If you need any help with packing or anything, let me know. I can make some time…" Steph said.

"Thanks. And if this person works out filling in with Dad, maybe once I'm back we can all sort of call on her to help when we need a break," Anna offered with a shrug.

Steph nodded silently as a wordless understanding passed between them. She'd extended an olive branch, and Anna had accepted it and offered one in return.

It wasn't perfect, but it was a start.

She blew out a pent-up breath and turned just as the bell on the door jangled again. This time, it wasn't a family member. It was Eva Hildebrand from the diner.

"You open yet or am I too early to get some cupcakes? Mo heard from Betty at the candle shop that they were delicious. He wants me to pick up two dozen to see how they go over with the lunch crowd."

Celia broke away from her circle and made a beeline toward Eva. "Mo wants to carry my cupcakes at the diner?" she asked, her eyes flashing with excitement.

"He does," Eva said, scratching her cap of dark gray hair. "And he says if they sell good and you give him a wholesale price, he'll set up a standing order every week."

Celia sent Steph and Anna a jubilant grin and slipped an arm around Eva. "We have about three minutes before we officially open." She handed her the price sheet. "Mo can take fifteen percent off those numbers if he's willing to commit to eight dozen or more a week."

Steph beamed with pride as she watched Cee-cee do her thing. She wasn't just a great baker—she was a natural businesswoman.

As Celia filled Eva's order, Anna and Steph straightened the already perfectly aligned white paper boxes behind the counter as they chatted with Celia's first and only employee, a teenager named Pete Mitchell who Max used to babysit. A few minutes later, Celia led Eva—loaded down with cupcakes—back toward the door before turning to face them.

"It's time! Eva, can you stay a minute for the official unveiling?" Celia asked.

Eva shrugged. "Sure."

They all headed out of the little shop, filing out the front door into the summer sunshine. Celia directed them to line up in a row as she stood proudly before the store, tears gleaming in her eyes.

"Everyone has been asking me about the shop's name, and a few of you have offered me suggestions. I've considered so many. Sweet Surprise, Death By Chocolate, and my personal favorite courtesy of Anna, Let Them Eat Cupcakes." Everyone chuckled at that as she continued. "It's been super hard to hide all the branded stuff I've been buying, but I really wanted to keep it a surprise. That might seem silly, given the choice I finally went with, but it means something to me," Celia said with a wobbly smile, gesturing toward the sign above the doorway, which was covered in a white sheet. "Thank you all for your support. Now, allow me to welcome you to…" She pulled on a rope that hung down from the sign, sending the sheet floating to the ground. "Cee-cee's Cupcakes!"

They broke out into applause, all except for Anna, who plugged her thumb and forefinger into her mouth and let out a joyous whistle.

"Thank you," Cee-cee said. "I wasn't sure what you'd think since I spent so much time on the name, but in the end, I wanted my name in it, because it's the first thing that is truly one-hundred-percent mine."

"It's perfect, Mom," Max said, engulfing her in a hug.

Gabe hugged them both. "We're so proud of you, Mom. You've been so strong."

"Congratulations, Cee-cee!" Steph called out, wiping a tear from the corner of her eye. She was proud of her, too.

She glanced at her watch, surprised to note that the grand opening had officially begun, but no one was there other than the family, Mick, and Eva.

Strange. They'd distributed flyers all week and Cee-cee was doing raffles, offering free lemonade and balloons to each customer, and had even hired a face painter.

"Whelp, I gotta go," Eva said. "Next stop is Nina Peterson's new place, Chip Off the Old Block cookie shop. They're having their grand opening today, as well, and she's got David Hasselhoff there signing autographs on old Baywatch posters from ten to twelve!" She tossed a quick wave over her shoulder before ambling off down the street.

Cee-cee's face fell like an undercooked soufflé, and Mick wrapped an arm around her. Anna took a step closer to Steph as they watched Eva leave, both of them stunned into silence.

Nina Peterson had opened a cookie shop? Stephanie hadn't seen a single flier or notice for it, and she would have paid attention. She'd never been one to pass up a good cookie.

"Well, crap," Anna finally said with a long sigh. "That was pretty slick. I don't know how you outdo the Hoff."

"Indeed," Steph muttered, wishing she had some stink bombs lying around. Why would a female business owner go out of her way to sabotage another female business owner just to be petty? Why couldn't they help each other and celebrate their successes together?

Stephanie lifted her chin, vowing to find out exactly that when she went over there. She and her sisters might not always get along, but she wouldn't let anyone else mess with them.

"Come on, Anna. We've got work to do."

Chapter Nineteen

Anna still had the taste of Cee-cee's s'mores cupcake in her mouth, which only made her more determined to help. Her sister was a fantastic baker, and she deserved success. Stephanie made their excuses to Cee-cee, who was in a huddle with Mick and her kids, trying to come up with a game plan to get more people through the doors.

Having gained their sister's blessing for the recon mission, they walked out of the shop and strode toward the pier with determination.

"I can't believe Nina Peterson opened a cookie shop," Stephanie said.

"I can't believe Nina Peterson hired the Hoff to sign autographs," Anna said. "I've loved him since *Night Rider*."

Stephanie swiveled to stare her down. "Anna, this is no time for you to let your crush on David Hasselhoff derail you. Sisters first."

Anna pushed out a sigh. Stephanie was right. "Why do you think Nina did this? I'd never heard a single mention of a cookie shop going in."

"I've heard her talk about opening a business," Stephanie said, "but it was years ago, and nothing ever came of it. I mean, there's no doubt Nina can bake. Her stuff always used to sell out at the church sales. Still, it seemed like she was more interested in dreaming big than doing anything about it, you know what I mean?" Her voice trailed off, soft and wispy.

Anna shot her sister a glance, trying to determine if Stephanie was talking about more than Nina. She knew Steph and Paul had always discussed their plans for the future. They'd talked about traveling more and possibly getting a winter home in Florida. Stephanie had thought about doing volunteer work for charities that provided care to animals in poverty-stricken areas. But after Paul's death, Stephanie had dropped all of that. All she seemed to do was work. It was like she was biding her time here on earth, waiting to join Paul.

"What are your dreams, Steph?" Anna blurted out.

Stephanie's steps faltered, but then she continued to plow ahead, a woman with a purpose. "Don't be ridiculous, Anna. This isn't the time for some heart to heart. We need to focus on saving Cee-cee's shop."

Anna grabbed her arm and pulled her to a halt. "I have two sisters and I care about both of them. What's your dream?"

"I'm fifty years old, Anna. I have three kids and a thriving veterinary practice. Being a vet was my dream. My life is full."

"Yeah," Anna said, her fingers still wrapped around her sister's arm. "You have a wonderful life, but what are *your dreams?*"

Stephanie started to say something then stopped and stared at Anna's mouth with a smirk. "You know, it's hard to take you seriously when you have icing smeared all over your face."

Anna licked her upper and lower lip. "Did I get it?"

Grinning, Stephanie pointed to the left corner of her own mouth. "You still have some here."

Anna's tongue swiped at the sugary remnants.

"Got it," Stephanie said, then started walking again.

"Steph…" Anna called after her, realizing her sister had used the art of distraction to get out of answering. She'd always been good at that. Anna was getting rusty.

"I have dreams," Anna said, catching up to her. "Cee-cee has dreams. Why can't you have new ones?"

"Cee-cee didn't have this dream of owning a cupcake shop until a few months ago. Before Nate left, it wasn't even on her radar."

"Good for Cee-cee for rolling with the punches and taking a new path with gusto." Anna grabbed Stephanie's wrist and tugged her sister next to the curb, letting a family pass. "You took a heck of a punch, Steph. A mind-numbing, soul-sucking, *terrible* punch." Her voice broke. "We all did. We loved Paul, too."

Tears filled Stephanie's eyes, but Anna took it as a good sign that she hadn't bolted yet. "It's okay to accept that your path changed. It's okay to pick a new one."

A tear slid down Stephanie's cheek. "But I still love him."

"Oh, honey," Anna forced out past the lump in her throat. "That's okay. You probably always will. Paul was a really great guy and you were so lucky to have him. Look at who poor Cee-cee got stuck with for thirty some years."

Both sisters released a chuckle.

"Paul died, Steph," Anna said, grabbing her sister's other wrist, "but *you* didn't. You're still here, living, breathing. Loving. You deserve to have dreams, too."

More tears streamed down Stephanie's face. "I wasn't very nice to him when he left that day."

Anna scrunched her face in confusion. "What?"

"The day he left… He asked me to come with him, but I refused. I made some snarky comment about one of us needing to work."

Anna's heart sank to her toes as she tried to imagine how much that must have weighed on her sister. "Oh, Stephanie…"

"I should have taken the day off and gone with him. If I had, he might not have…"

Anna pulled her sister into her arms. "No. None of that. What ifs never helped a thing. What's done is done. And you were a great wife to Paul. He knew how you felt about him." To Anna's surprise, her sister started to cry harder.

"I don't think I even said I love you," she cried into Anna's shoulder.

Anna held her tighter, shooting an evil glare to a couple walking past and openly staring at them. "It's okay."

"No. It's not. I should know something like that. I should have…"

Anna held Stephanie's arms and leaned back to search her face. "They're just words. Sure, they're important words, and we want and need to hear them, but how many times a day did you used to tell him you love him?"

Stephanie's brow furrowed. "At least once or twice. Maybe more."

"And how many times did you *show* him that you loved him? Because I saw proof of it every time you two were together, and I saw proof that he loved you, too." Her voice broke as tears stung her eyes. "And boy did he love you."

Stephanie's chin quivered.

Anna gave her a soft smile. "Don't you see, Steph? It didn't matter if you said the words. He already knew."

Stephanie bit her lower lip and glanced down at the ground, more tears streaming down her cheeks.

The timing of this conversation sucked, but Anna didn't really care, as long as her sister took some of it to heart. As long as it created a bridge between the two of them.

Taking a deep breath, Stephanie wiped her face with her fingertips and squared her shoulders. "You've given me a lot to think about."

"I love you, Steph. You deserve happiness."

She took a step back and said, "And Cee-cee does, too, so let's get to the bottom of this."

They continued toward the pier, and by the time they approached the crowd on the sidewalk ahead, Stephanie's face was less splotchy and her eyes not quite as red.

"Do I look okay?" she asked, swiping at her cheeks again.

"You look like you've had too much sun and pollen. Otherwise, you look fine," Anna said.

Stephanie's mouth dropped open, then she quickly closed it. "That's not very reassuring, but at least I know I can always rely on you to tell it like it is."

"You're fine," she said, giving her attention to the fifty or so people waiting in line. Something about this whole to-do didn't smell right, and it wasn't the odor of fresh fish rolling off the harbor.

Anna gave the crowd a sideways nod. "I'm goin' in."

"Be on your best behavior, Anna," Stephanie admonished. "This is a fact-finding mission."

Anna propped her hand on her hip. "Define best behavior."

Stephanie seemed to fumble over what to say, finally settling on, "Ask yourself 'what would Cee-cee do?'"

"Old Cee-cee or new?"

Stephanie laughed. "New. Which means we're in deep trouble."

Anna winked. "Yep." Then, before her sister could stop her, she started nudging her way through the crowd filled with kids and parents. It struck her that there were an inordinate number of middle-aged women.

So the Hoff had worked his magic.

Chip Off the Old Block was smaller than the cupcake shop, but there were certainly more people inside. The decor looked half-done, which meant Nina had likely taken shortcuts to get this place open on the same day as Cee-cee's.

Interesting.

"You're cutting in line," a woman called out, and Anna immediately recognized the voice.

Maryanne.

Anna turned to face her nemesis, wondering how in the world they'd gotten to this place. They were grown women, for heaven's sake. Why were they falling into a pattern best left behind in high school?

"Just checking the place out," Anna said with a forced smile.

"You mean checking out the competition?"

"Funny," Anna said, glancing around. It looked like most of the people crowding the store were there for the Hoff, who sat in a corner in the back, looking overwhelmed by the crush of bodies. Two guards flanked him, keeping the line back. "He was a nice touch."

"What can I say?" Maryanne gloated. "I know people."

So Maryanne was behind all of this.

A teenage girl walked past, carrying a tray of cookie samples. Anna snatched a piece and popped it into her mouth, fully expecting it to be mediocre. She was shocked at the delicious blend of flavors.

Maryanne's brows lifted with a smirk. "Good, aren't they?"

Anna scowled, but at the moment, she was more worried about David Hasselhoff. A group of women had rushed him, and his guards were trying to keep them away. "You might want to worry more about protecting the Hoff."

"Who?" she asked.

Anna shoved her way to the front of the crowd, then turned around to face them, releasing an ear-piercing whistle.

The crowd stilled and quieted.

"Ladies!" Anna called out. "You'll all get your turn. The Hoff will sign autographs for everyone!"

One of the guards leaned into her ear. "He's only here for another hour."

"Really?" There was no way everyone in line would get through to see him.

"Ladies!" she called out again, going with a different tactic. She moved to the side and gestured toward him. "The Hoff is a national treasure! If you want your turn to see him, then get into a single-file line and patiently wait your turn or he'll be forced to leave."

A groan of dismay swept through the room.

Anna held up her hands. "But if you can wait patiently, he'll stay and sign photos for you. And, once you're done here, come on over to Cee-cee's Cupcakes for some free lemonade and face painting for the kids!" To her surprise, the crowd listened. While Maryanne looked on with a glare, her arms crossed over her chest, Anna organized the crowd into two lines—people who just wanted cookies, and those who were more interested in autographs.

When everyone was sorted, Anna cut to the front, and the Hoff smiled at her. "Thank you."

Anna whipped out her cell phone and turned her back to him to get a selfie. To her surprise, he leaned in and kissed her on the cheek. Her skin flushed.

"Can I get an autograph?" she asked.

"After that? You bet." He grabbed a black and white 8 x 10 to sign with his Sharpie.

"Not there," she said. "Here." Then she stuck her chest out and grinned at his raised brows. "I mean the shirt, not the boob, Mr. Hasselhoff."

He chuckled. "It wouldn't be the first time." He finished his signature on the shirt, just over her collarbone. "What's your name?"

"Anna. Anna Sullivan," she said, her stomach fluttering. She'd been calm until he'd asked for her name.

"Well, thank you, Anna Sullivan. If you ever need a job as a handler, let me know."

"Thanks," she said with a laugh. "I will."

She pushed past the now-organized crowd and found her sister on the sidewalk, shaking her head with a grin.

"What?" Anna asked. "It was the Hoff! I couldn't show up and not get his autograph."

"One could say you were aiding and abetting the enemy."

"I was protecting a national treasure. Besides, the sooner everyone gets his autograph, the sooner they can move on to Cee-cee's place." She pulled a face. "But I gotta admit it. The cookies are good."

"You bought one?" Steph asked with a scowl.

"No, it was a free sample, but Nina's cookies are really good, and her shop is next to the pier. We need to consider that—"

Stephanie held up her hands, cringing. "Don't say it."

"Cee-cee's shop might be in trouble."

Chapter Twenty

"Whew," Cee-cee said as she sank against the countertop with a happy sigh. She'd just gotten back from walking Tilly a few minutes before and was surprised to find that, although her feet ached, she felt totally energized despite the breakneck pace of the day. "That was a seriously crazy afternoon! How many people you think came through?" she asked Pete, who was busy wiping down the near-empty cases with a cloth.

"Felt like a million," he said with a lopsided grin. "I swear, seemed like the second I thought the line was getting shorter, more people piled in."

It hadn't started out that way, though. In fact, she'd been bitterly disappointed, at first. When the scheduled opening time had come and gone without any fanfare, she'd started to worry, something that had only escalated when her sisters returned to tell her about Chip Off the Old Block. It didn't feel like a coincidence that Nina had opened a cookie shop on the same day, especially since she hadn't put out any advance publicity. To Cee-cee's relief, customers had started streaming over from Nina's once the signing was over. Still...it was all very strange.

The bell above the door jangled and she straightened, a welcoming smile on her face. Eva Hildebrand stepped in, wearing her apron from her lunch shift at the diner.

"Whelp, you did it, girlie. Those cupcakes went like...*hot*cakes, ha!" she chortled, charmed with her own little joke. "We sold out and now the early bird dinner crowd is pissed they're gone. Mo sent me by to put in an order for eight dozen more to cover us for the weekend, and a standing order for the rest of the season. We'll have to reevaluate once the tourists clear out, of course."

"Of course," Cee-cee said, excitement bubbling through her as thoughts of Nina and her cookie shop faded. This was exactly the type of business she needed. Weekly orders that she could count on would be her bread and butter.

She and Eva stood at the counter and talked over the flavor options for a few minutes and then Eva was on her way.

"I think we're done here for the day, Pete. I've got two more batches baking that I need to wait on for tomorrow, but then I'll be heading out, too. See you tomorrow at nine?"

The teen nodded and shot her a grin. "You bet. I wound up with twenty-six dollars just in tips today. I'm going to make a killing at this job."

Cee-cee watched him go, praying he was right.

Today had been a pretty strong day overall. She still had to go through the credit card receipts and reconcile the register, but she was fairly certain she'd even made an unexpected profit despite the giveaways, raffles, and freebies. How would she fare off-season with another bakery so close by, likely splitting the loyalties of the townies? Sure, one specialized in cupcakes, the other in cookies, but both sold sweet treats. Indulgences.

Only time would tell, but she was going to have to make some big headway with event venues and area restaurants if she wanted to get a leg up.

She made for the door to lock it, but it swung open before she got there. Mick stood there with a wide grin on his face as he peered past her to survey the display cases.

"Just like I thought. They cleaned this place out like a bunch of locusts."

She laughed and moved toward him, a warm glow settling over her. "Yeah, once they started coming it was pretty much nonstop. My feet are killing me, not that I'm complaining. I'll take sore feet over a bunch of leftover cupcakes any day."

He held out his arms and she slipped into his embrace, rolling up onto her tiptoes for a kiss. This thing with Mick was getting to feel like part of her new normal. She liked it. A lot.

"If you're nice, I might be willing to trade a foot rub for any leftovers," Mick murmured, swiping a stray lock of hair from her eyes. "When I left to do that job over on Cobblestone Lane, I got so busy I forgot to eat lunch."

She took his hand and tugged him toward the door to the basement.

"Lucky for you, I bought myself a massive turkey sandwich from the deli that I didn't have time to eat. What do you say we share it while I wait for my devil's food cupcakes to bake? Then we can go upstairs and I'll take you up on your offer."

His eyes lit up as he followed her lead. They chatted easily as they ate and Celia puttered around the kitchen, prepping for the following day. Once the ovens were off and the cupcakes were stored to cool, they made their way up to her apartment.

"I'm still a little weirded out about the whole Nina thing," she admitted once she'd fed Tilly and sat on the couch beside Mick. She slipped off her shoes and folded her legs beneath her. "I don't know her that well, but we've always been friendly...or so I thought. Seems like bad business to have her Grand Opening the same day as mine, unless there was some compelling reason, although I can't imagine what that might be..."

"You sure it's not a coincidence?"

"It could be," she said with a shrug, "but my gut tells me it isn't. Especially not with Maryanne involved."

Mick sat back, patting his lap invitingly, and she leaned back and draped her legs on him. This wasn't new. For the past week, they'd been getting more and more familiar. Casual kisses, easy caresses and absent-minded touching while they walked, talked, or watched TV together. They always found reasons to be close, even when they were working on the apartment or in the shop. She would feed him a bite of her new flavor combo, or he would brush a paint chip from her hair. They were starting to become a real couple and she had to wonder if it felt as right to him as it did to her.

Then he started to rub her feet and she couldn't think at all.

"Oh my gosh, you should make a career change. Those hands are seriously magic," she said with a laughing groan.

"Happy to oblige, ma'am, but these hands are only licensed for two feet, and I've got both of them in my lap right now."

She let out a happy sigh and began to relax, letting the cares of the day slip away. Until Nina Peterson's face flickered through her mind again and she pushed herself upright.

"You know what, Mick? I'm not going to sit here and stew, wondering what was on Nina's mind. I'm going to give her a call and ask her. The old Celia would've tucked her tail between her legs and stayed silent, worried she'd done something to offend. But that's not me anymore. We're both grown, intelligent women and there is no reason we shouldn't put our cards on the table."

Mick shot her an admiring glance and nodded. "I think that's a great idea. If she does have a problem with you, at least you can try to sort it out. If not, then you'll know all this worry was for nothing."

Mind made up, she snatched her cell phone from her apron pocket and did a quick search for Nina's number. She found it on Linked Up after only a few minutes and quickly dialed before she could talk herself out of it.

This was the mature thing to do, she reminded herself as the phone rang on the other end.

"Hello?" a female voice said warily.

"Nina? Hi, this is Celia Burrows."

There was a long pause before Nina replied. "Hi, Celia. I heard you had your shop opening today. Congratulations!"

She didn't *sound* angry or bitter, but maybe she was just a really good actress.

"Thanks so much. Actually, that's what I was calling about. I hadn't even realized you were opening a store and then suddenly there it was, launching on the same day as mine." She paused, trying to word this next part as diplomatically as possible. "I couldn't help but wonder if I should take this personally or if it was just a coincidence?"

Nina let out a low hiss. "Oh, Celia, I'm so sorry about that. I didn't mean for it to play out this way. I've been batting the idea of the cookie shop around for years, and then Maryanne Brown approached me a couple of weeks ago and mentioned that she had a cousin who had a space for lease at the pier. It was a really great deal, so I leapt at it. Things just fell into place from there. She found a handyman to help me fix it up and even talked her sister's brother-in-law, who's friends with David Hasselhoff's agent," she said in a breathless rush. "I went along with the whirlwind, and before I knew it, she'd gotten him booked and all. I had no idea about your opening until yesterday, and by then, it was too late to change it. Can you forgive me?"

Cee-cee let that sink in for a second before replying. "There's nothing to forgive, Nina." At least, Nina had done nothing wrong. Maryanne was another story. What was that woman's problem? Celia knew she had issues with Anna for some reason, but it had seemed like stupid, petty baggage from high school. And while Anna always said Maryanna was jealous of Cee-cee's happy marriage and Nate's success, that had all blown up now. It seemed crazy for this woman to still have it out for her. None of that was Nina's fault, though. She'd just gotten caught in the crossfire. "In fact, I was hoping we could maybe talk about doing some cross-promotion, especially once the busy season is over?"

"I would love that," Nina said, the relief evident in her voice.

Cee-cee caught sight of Mick, who was giving her a thumbs-up with his brows raised in question. She nodded and shot him a thumbs up in reply before continuing.

"Let's make time to talk next week or the week after, once we've settled into our routines. How does that sound?"

"Perfect. I have to say, I heard several customers talking in passing, and word on the street is that your shop is an experience. The customers loved the decorating nook and the tables and chairs and the view. We really might be looking at two different niches in the long run. And your sisters were a hoot. Anna came in and made sure everyone knew you were having a grand opening today, too," she added with a chuckle. "I don't have any siblings and my friends are mostly of the Maryanne Brown ilk. It must be nice to have that kind of selfless support."

Cee-cee cringed a little and laughed. "Yeah, they're great...most of the time." They'd told her a bit about the cookie shop, but they hadn't mentioned Anna's announcement.

"Anyway, I really appreciate you taking my call and I look forward to talking soon."

Nina thanked her in response, and Cee-cee disconnected, feeling like she'd dumped an anvil off her chest.

"Feel better?" Mick asked.

"I do. It wasn't even really Nina. Maryanne Carpenter Brown's the one with a chip on her shoulder, and I can't decide if I should give her the satisfaction of fighting back, or if I should let my success do the talking."

Mick leaned in and pressed his mouth to hers in a soft, slow kiss that had her toes curling.

"I say put a pin in it and decide tomorrow morning."

Cee-cee bit her bottom lip, coming to a decision in that instant. "After we have breakfast?" she asked softly, her voice full of promise. She and Mick hadn't taken their relationship to that level despite their outward intimacy, and Cee-cee realized with a start that she was ready for the next step.

More than ready.

Mick's face filled with affection as he pulled her into his arms. "Ah, Cee-cee. You don't need to bribe me with food. You're all I need."

Chapter Twenty-One

Stephanie stood outside her father's front door, steeling her back before she walked in. The last few times she'd come by to bring Pop his dinner had gone well, but she still couldn't relax. There were too many years of awkwardness to overcome for one or two visits to fix everything. Too much water under the bridge.

Pasting a smile on her face, she rapped on the door, then pushed it open. "Hey, Pop! I hope you're hungry!"

A shiver of fear ran down her back when he didn't answer. Had he run off again?

"Pop?" she called out, setting the takeout bag on the kitchen table. She checked the entire downstairs and then heard footsteps above head. They'd specifically told him not to go up there...

Of course, that was exactly where she found him, after going through the still-open door to the bedroom.

"Pop?" she called out, softer this time when she saw him sitting on an overturned wooden crate with a photo album in his lap.

He glanced up at her, and the softness in his eyes hardened over. "I know what you're gonna say, but I—"

She had to admit, anger was her first reaction, but mostly out of fear for his safety, closely followed by her impatience at his independent streak. The particular album in his lap pushed her irritation away, though. These were photos that dated back to the early days of her parents' relationship.

He was looking at photos of Mom.

Picking her way around the furniture and boxes, she said as she moved toward him, "We just worry about you, Pop."

"I'm fine in my own home," he snapped, then turned back to the page, his anger turning to sorrow.

She squatted next to him, tears stinging her eyes as she looked at the photographs of her mother as a young woman. There she was in her parents' backyard with two friends and her younger sister, all of them reclining on lounge chairs. In another photo, she sat opposite Pop, both of them so young they looked like babies, although surely they were in their late teens. And in another, her parents were with a group of friends, sitting in the bed of a pickup truck at a drive-in movie.

They looked so happy and carefree, nothing like the stressed and weary parents she remembered. Of course, these photos had been taken before they had three daughters within four years. Her father had struggled to make ends meet for the family—a difficult task in the midst of a major recession, especially since he'd lacked any marketable job skills. She'd never stopped to think what life had been like for her parents back then, trying to keep their small house and provide for three kids.

"Your mother was a beauty," he said, his voice breaking. His thumb rubbed the edge of a photo of her mother. She was sitting on a cliff overlooking the ocean, but she was beaming at the camera or, more likely, the man behind it.

"Yeah, she was. Right up until the day she died," Stephanie said past the lump in her throat. Her mother had always taken great care in her appearance. She'd told Stephanie more than once that she liked to look her best for her husband. Her night-care routine could have filled a book. Stephanie had never fussed with any of that, and it had bothered her that her mother cared so much. Paul had always made Stephanie feel she was perfect and desirable just as she was, wrinkles and all.

"I miss her," Pop said, and the brokenness in the voice of the proud, stern man she knew so well cracked the guard she'd firmly built around her heart.

"I miss her, too."

He turned his head to glance at her, and Stephanie was surprised to see tears in his eyes. "She loved you, too, Stuffing."

The burning in her eyes and her throat increased at his use of the nickname he'd given her when she was in preschool.

He returned his gaze to the album and turned the page. This one held a few candid photos of their wedding, although Stephanie knew there was an album with their actual wedding photos in another box.

"Did you know she wanted to be a nurse?" he asked, turning the page again, not interested in studying the reminders of his wedding.

"She'd mentioned it." In fact, Stephanie had encouraged her mother to go back to school once Anna hit middle school, reassuring her that they wouldn't burn the house down in her absence.

But her mother wouldn't hear of it. "My place is here, taking care of you girls and your father." Then she'd smile and say, "Whatever would he do if he came home after a hard day of work and there was no dinner on the table?"

Suddenly, Stephanie realized where part of her resentment toward her father came from—his misogynistic attitudes about male and female roles had kept her mother from living her dream. Just like he'd tried to keep Stephanie from living hers.

Her fondness for her father dried up like a raindrop on a hot summer day. "Your dinner's downstairs. We should probably get down there so you can eat it before it gets cold."

His brow furrowed as he studied her. "I know you think I did your mother wrong."

Stephanie rocked back on her heels in shock. Her father wasn't usually so astute. But she wasn't sure how to handle this—sweep it under the rug like she usually did or finally address it? Was her father strong enough to handle it?

Was *she?*

"Pop," she said in warning.

"I loved her. I loved her more than anyone or anything," he said, his voice breaking. "I loved her as much as your Paul loved you."

That unexpected insight brought a rush of tears to her eyes.

"You know what I find so strange?" he asked.

"What?" she responded, despite herself.

"Out of our entire family, you and I should be the ones who understand each other the most, yet you can't stand to come see me."

"That's not true," Stephanie said in defense, an automatic response that popped out before she could admit to herself he was right.

"It is. I may be old, and I might be forgetful from time to time, but I ain't blind. I can see it, plain as day."

She didn't answer. She hated to lie to him again.

"Maybe you have other reasons for not coming around. I know you always liked seeing your mother more than me," he said, sounding thoughtful. "I expect seeing me also reminds you of what you lost when your Paul died. But I know you've got it in your head that I didn't treat your mother right." His voice cracked and he swallowed. "I know you thought we were old-fashioned, your mother staying home when a lot of women went out to get jobs, but that was her decision. I gave her what she wanted."

Something about the last line caught her attention. "What do you mean you gave her what she wanted?"

"I don't want to speak ill of your mother, Stephanie."

She blinked in shock. "What are you talking about?"

He grimaced. "Back when you girls were in your early teens, when things were so tight I wasn't sure I'd have enough gas to get to work, let alone buy you girls new shoes, your mother was offered a job at the local nursing home. It wasn't much pay, but it was taking care of patients like she'd always wanted, even if it meant sometimes changing bed pans. But she turned it down, saying she didn't want to leave you girls, even if you were in school all day, and even if we were barely scraping by. I let her stay home, because that was what she wanted."

Stephanie stared at her father in horror. How had she never known any of this?

How had she gotten everything so wrong?

"Pop, I'm sorry."

"You've got nothing to be sorry about," he said with a wave of his hand. He closed the album and set it in the open box. "Did you bring me pork chops?"

"Yeah," she said, her gaze on the box, but she quickly came to her senses. Getting to her feet, she offered him a hand to help him up. "I can bring the albums downstairs if you want to look at them again."

He started shuffling to the door. "No. I think I'm ready to let her go."

AS STEPHANIE DROVE HOME, she thought about her unexpected evening with her father, realizing that things weren't always what they appeared to be. Her parents' marriage was proof-positive of that. A good lesson to remember.

Her phone rang as she was pulling into the driveway, and she was surprised to see it was Cee-cee.

"I thought you were going out with Mick tonight," Stephanie said as she answered.

"I am, but I thought I'd call to check on how your visit with Pop went."

Stephanie tried to keep her aggravation in check. "You mean you're checking up on me."

"Noooo…" Cee-cee drew out the word. "Pop seemed out of it more than usual when I dropped by to bring him his lunch. He was in the backyard looking for Mittens. It took me five minutes to convince him to come back inside, but I had to lie to him and tell him that Mittens was at the Fishers' house and they would bring her home later. Was he okay tonight?"

Mittens had been the girls' cat when they were in elementary school. "Uh… no," she said as she got out of her car and walked into the kitchen. "He was fine. More lucid than I'd seen him in weeks."

Her own pack of animals greeted her at the door—all rescues from the clinic. A black lab, a French bulldog whose owners hadn't been able to keep up with its many medical issues, and a calico cat with a missing back leg. She bent over to give them all love.

"We might need to make some hard decisions," Cee-cee said. "I'm not sure our current arrangement will keep working."

Stephanie opened her refrigerator to figure out her dinner options, resorting to an already open bottle of wine and a leftover block of Colby Jack cheese. "The next step is assisted living, whether it's in his house or somewhere else." But that *somewhere else* would likely be one of their homes. Cee-cee had just moved into a second floor apartment and Anna's place was even smaller, not to mention she was leaving for three or four months.

Which left Stephanie's house.

Stephanie pushed out a sigh. "I'm not sure we need to address this yet. And I definitely need to do it when I'm not this exhausted."

"But we should discuss it before Anna leaves."

"Agreed." Before she hung up, she quickly added, "Hey, Cee-cee, did you know that Mom was offered a job at a local nursing home when we were preteens?" She figured if any of them would know, it would be Cee-cee, the oldest.

"No," she answered in shock. "Where did you hear that?"

"Pop."

After a moment's hesitation, Cee-cee said, "Are you sure his mind wasn't off?"

Stephanie shook her head, even if her sister couldn't see her. "No. He was totally there."

"I had no idea."

"Neither did I," Stephanie said. "Have a good night."

"You too, Steph."

Stephanie turned on the TV and grabbed some crackers to accompany her wine and cheese, but her mind was tumbling over everything her father had told her. Anna, too. One thing stuck out at her more than the rest.

It was time to let Paul go.

She would always love him, but it was time to re-engage in life.

She'd start by taking his things out of their closet.

She had the next day, Sunday, off, but once the idea took root, she couldn't ignore it. If she didn't start at once, she risked losing her nerve. So she found an empty box in the garage and brought a roll of trash bags and walked into the closet, armed with a fresh bottle of wine and her determination.

She could do this.

She was crying as she took the first shirt off the hanger, burying her nose into the fabric. His scent had long since disappeared, but she'd still hoped to catch one last whiff of him to tide her over for eternity. She cradled it to her chest, as though holding him one last time, then tossed it onto the floor into what she designated the giveaway pile.

The next hour went faster than she'd expected, and the task became easier as she sorted through his clothing, shoes, and accessories. Most went into the giveaway pile, some ratty things like old T-shirts and underwear went into the trash pile, but she left the few precious items she was allowing herself to keep on hangers and in one drawer.

By the time she'd bagged up the giveaway and trash items, it was nearly midnight, but she felt a huge weight lift off her shoulders. She'd expected to feel guilty about letting Paul go, but instead, she felt lighter, like she was ready to face a new chapter in her life.

She considered leaving the keep items until the morning, but she worried inertia would kick in again, so she carried the few things she'd chosen to her bed and went through them one by one, loving on them before folding them up and putting them carefully into the box. It was a mishmash of items—a tie with bananas printed on navy blue polyester the kids had given him for Christmas one year. An old T-shirt she'd hated but he'd loved, which he'd sometimes worn just to aggravate her. The dress shirt she'd gotten him for an important work dinner. The dinner had gone well and he'd called it his lucky shirt ever since. And finally, his tweed jacket—his favorite.

She held on to the jacket for several seconds, wrapping her fingers around the fabric and catching the faintest smell of him. Was it her imagination? She didn't care, holding on tighter and letting her tears fall again. He'd worn it to work the day before his accident, so she searched the pockets, hoping for a snapshot of his last full day.

One pocket was empty, but the other held a small, double-folded piece of paper. Setting the jacket on the bed, she opened the note and read in a handwriting she didn't recognize, *I'm getting it tomorrow. Meet me on the pier at six.*

An icy cold sensation swept over her as she stared at it. Had the note come from the day before Paul's death? Who had written it, what were they getting, and most of all, why were they meeting Paul?

Her mind latched on to the mystery, looking for ways to make it fit her narrative of the circumstances of his death, but in the end, what did it matter? Paul was dead and he was never coming back.

Still, she found she couldn't bring herself to throw it away. She refolded it and tucked it into the top drawer of Paul's nightstand, realizing she needed to clean that out, as well.

It would have to wait for another day, though. Stephanie had let go of enough.

But when she closed her eyes in bed that night, it wasn't the things she'd let go of that plagued her thoughts. It was the one thing she'd found.

Chapter Twenty-Two

Anna peered out the windshield of her car as she pulled into the lot of Beckett's Towing, pleased to see Beckett seated at a desk in front of a pile of papers. She popped the car into park and snatched up the envelope on the dashboard, not bothering to turn off the ignition. She only had a minute, but with less than two weeks until her departure date, she knew if she didn't do this now, it wouldn't get done, and this was important. After all, Beckett was the one who'd given her the idea in the first place.

She exited the car and made her way to the door of the little office, waving as Beckett looked up and met her gaze with a smile.

"Hey," she said as she stepped in. "Hope I'm not interrupting."

"Not at all," he said, shoving the papers away with a sigh. "Actually, I'm happy for the break. My bookkeeper is on maternity leave, and I have to admit this isn't exactly my forte. How have you been? Did you ever make it out to see the puffins?"

She held up the envelope and waved it in the air. "Actually, that's why I'm here. I can't stay, but I wanted to make sure you know I'm a woman of my word." She tossed the envelope on the desk between them, surprised by the sudden rush of nerves. She was a great photographer. Not just by her own estimation—her work was sought after by countless magazines and websites. Why was she so apprehensive about this picture?

Beckett tugged the flap of the envelope open and slid the image out. It was of a mother puffin nuzzling her fuzzy little baby, her brightly colored beak and every detail of her face showcased in perfect clarity.

"I know I said I'd let you choose, but for some reason this one stood out to me, and I wanted you to have it. If you'd rather another, it's no problem..."

Beckett's face said it all, but that didn't stop him from raving. "You're a genius. Seriously. It's so perfect it doesn't even look real. How long did it take you to get this shot?"

"That one?" she asked with a chuckle. "About three hours. But I took six hundred others during that time that I archived. What can I say? Patience is a virtue." Her face felt warm and she cleared her throat as she jerked a thumb toward her car. "Anyway, I've got to head out. I'm leaving for an assignment soon and I have tons of loose ends to tie up before I go. I just wanted to fulfill my promise, so there you have it. An Anna Sullivan exclusive."

"Exclusive? You mean you aren't going to sell it anywhere else?" he asked, his brows caving into a frown. "Anna, that's too much..."

"It's nothing. The least I can do. I wouldn't have even thought to go to the sanctuary if it hadn't been for you. If you decide to put it in a frame or something, let me know and I can sign it."

For a second, it seemed like he was going to argue further, but then he just smiled.

"Thank you. It really means a lot. And I definitely want it signed when you get back." He cocked his head and regarded her, expression solemn. "When will that be, anyway?"

"It's a long one. At least three months, likely more."

"I hope we run into each other when you get back, then," Beckett said simply.

She nodded and gave him one last wave before rushing out to her car.

As she made the drive toward the beach where she was scheduled to meet Cee-cee and Stephanie, she couldn't help but note that, for the first time, her impending departure felt bittersweet. She was worried about the situation with Pop, but it wasn't just that. The usual itch she felt to get a move on had strangely begun to fade this time. Was it just some sort of Stockholm Syndrome setting in? Maybe she'd wanted to leave for so long she'd come out the other side, brainwashed into thinking she wanted to stay in Bluebird Bay?

"Or are you just getting old and tired, like Katie the yoga chippy suggested?" she muttered at her reflection in the rear-view mirror.

She let out a sigh and hit the blinker right as she pulled into the public beach parking lot.

It was a cooler day, mid-seventies, and the breeze was blowing but the sun was bright. Perfect. She grabbed her beach bag and headed toward the spot right in front of the lifeguard station where she'd arranged to meet her sisters.

When she got there, Steph and Cee-cee were already there, reclined on a pair of chaise lounges, both sporting chic, one-piece suits.

"What's up, ladies?" she chirped, setting down her beach bag.

"Hey, sis," Steph said, shielding her eyes from the sun as she peered up at her. "Cee-cee brought a chaise for you, too," she added, pointing at the folded-up chair on the sand between them.

"Thanks. And I brought some grapes and bottled water in a freezer bag," she replied, shaking her duffel.

She set down her things and stripped off her T-shirt and shorts to reveal her new yellow bikini.

Cee-cee let out a low whistle. "Hot stuff, look at you! I remember having a stomach like that," she murmured with a wistful chuckle.

Steph let out a snort. "Lucky you, because I don't! Even before kids, my abs were shy."

Anne unpretzeled the chair and laid down in the sun between her sisters with a happy sigh. This was nice, being with them just for the sheer joy of it. None of them had anything to do or anywhere to be. As she took in the view of the water and the cheery blue sky, Anna shivered, thinking of how cold it would be in the Arctic.

She cut that thought short, refusing to dwell on the sudden uncertainty that had been gnawing at her lately. She was here now, and she was going to enjoy it.

"How are things at the shop?"

"Great," Cee-cee said with a grin. "The weekend was crazy, and last Monday and Tuesday were a little slower, which is why I was okay with leaving Pete to mind the store this afternoon. But between walk-ins, kids events, orders from the diner and a couple of other restaurants, I can't complain." She snapped her fingers and pointed at Anna. "Speaking of which, I've been meaning to ask you something and I keep forgetting. What's the origin of Maryanne's beef with us? I called Nina after the opening last week and she basically said the whole thing was Maryanne's idea. This can't seriously be over some stupid firecracker in high school, or some petty jealousy about my now defunct marriage? I barely know the woman, but I remember you saying she didn't like you and then there being some tension over Stephanie's cheer position in high school. How did it all start?"

Anna frowned and shrugged. "I wish I knew. We were barely acquaintances, and then one day it was like a switch flipped. She's seemed to have it out for me ever since. In fact, I'm convinced she dropped Stephanie from the cheer pyramid that time just to stick it to me. I don't think about it much, but now that you mention it, it's a little strange. We didn't even run in the same circles."

Steph rolled onto her stomach and settled back into her chaise. "Well, if she keeps it up, we're going to have to have a talk with her. This is getting a little ridiculous. She's talking junk about Cee-cee's kids at the diner, knowing you'd overhear, and then this whole grand opening war." She turned her attention to Cee-cee. "Were you and Nina able to talk things out?"

"We were. We're planning to help promote each other once we're both settled in. She was really lovely about it. In fact, I'd like to invite her to one of our sisters' lunches in the next few weeks." Cee-cee shot Anna a quick glance. "Or at least when you and I go to lunch, Steph, since Anna won't be here."

Guilt mixed with a bit of unexpected jealousy shot through Anna and she cleared her throat.

"Actually, I need to talk to you guys about that. I know I said I'd arrange for someone to cover my shifts with Pop, but I still don't have it all hammered out. I'm waiting for—"

"No." Cee-cee popped up from her chaise like a Jack-in-the-box. "Nope, not gonna happen, Anna. I supported you going and even said I'd help smooth things over with Steph. I only asked you for one thing—one!" she said, thrusting her finger in the air and stammering, she was so angry. "And now here we are, less than two weeks from you leaving, and you have nothing in place. Do you realize the position that puts me in?"

Anna swallowed hard and tried to cut in, but Cee-cee wasn't having it.

"I gave up my whole identity for a person I loved. I'll never do it again, not even for you guys. I'm not asking you to stay, Anna. I'm not asking you to give up your whole life for Dad, Steph. I'm asking you both to figure out your crap and help. If that means interviewing candidates for a home nurse, then you'd better get started. Let me know when you've done that. Until then, I don't want to hear it."

Anna and Steph both stared at Celia in silence. As far as speeches went, it was a good one. If her goal had been to make Anna feel like a piece of crap, she'd definitely succeeded. She wanted to argue that she had someone in mind and was just waiting to nail it all down. She was trying her best. But there was no point in saying anything when she had nothing solid to tell her, because Cee-cee was right.

In the words of the great Yoda, do or do not do. There is no try.

"You're right. I messed up," Anna said softly. "And don't worry, I hear you loud and clear. I'm going to fix it...*before* I go. You have my word on that, Cee-cee."

"I...I appreciate that," Cee-cee said, slumping forward as if Anna had taken some of the wind out of her sails. "Sorry, I was geared up for a fight so I'm sort of at a loss as to what to do with all this adrenaline now," she admitted with a chuckle.

"And if the agency can't commit so quickly, let me know, Anna. I can pick up a couple of your shifts to cover the gap if need be," Steph said, rolling over and sitting up to get a water from Anna's bag, all casual-like.

"What did you just say?" Cee-cee asked, eyes narrowing suspiciously.

"I *said* I can pitch in a bit extra if need be. Geeze, Cee-cee, I thought you'd be happy."

"Why the change of heart?" Anna asked softly, studying her sister's face.

Steph shrugged self-consciously. "Me and Pop had a moment the other night when I was there. We bonded a little and I sort of realized I held some resentment toward him because I felt like he never let Mom have her own identity. We got to talking and he said Mom never really wanted to work. She loved being a mother so much, she wanted that to be her identity, even though it made things tight financially sometimes." Stephanie looked away, abashed. "It was a bit of a wake-up call for me. We still don't have a whole lot to talk about, but I'm willing to put in the effort to find some common ground with him. He even convinced me it was time to start cleaning out Paul's things."

Anna nodded slowly and reached out to take Steph's hand. "That's so great. I think that's going to be super cathartic for you."

"I started the night before last, and it was." The tiny muscle in her jaw began to tick and Anna cocked her head. That was Steph's 'Houston, we have a problem' tell.

"But?" Cee-cee urged, clearly sensing it, too.

"But I found something in Paul's pocket. A note in handwriting I didn't recognize talking about meeting him at the pier."

"What did it say, exactly?" Anna pressed.

Steph didn't bother pretending she hadn't memorized it. "It said 'I'm getting it tomorrow. Meet me on the pier at six.'"

Anna and Cee-cee locked gazes and both shrugged.

"That does seem weird now that he's passed away, and on a boat, no less, but there's probably a perfectly reasonable explanation. Could've been from someone who sold him something for the boat, maybe, or one of the shops at the pier," Cee-cee said lightly.

"You'll probably never figure it out, Steph," Anna added, "because it wasn't important. The important thing here is what we do know…and we know Paul loved you to pieces. You were his soulmate. He didn't just say it. He showed you, each and every day. Don't let some silly piece of paper make you forget that. Just let it go, okay?"

Anna was talking straight logic. That was exactly the right advice. But at the same time, she couldn't help thinking she wouldn't have been able to forget about it if it had been her. An unsolved mystery was like a flame and she was the moth. Even now she wanted to pepper her sister with more questions. What kind of paper was it? Cursive or printed? What piece of clothing had she found it in?

But all that would do was upset Steph further, so she zipped her lips.

The rest of the day was one of the best she could remember. Now that they'd cleared the air about Pop, Cee-cee seemed much more carefree. And, despite the strange note, Steph seemed to take Anna's advice and let it go. They spent the afternoon swimming, working on their tans, and munching on grapes. When the sun began to fade, they dressed and headed over the Steph's house for a meal of wine, cheese, and a crusty loaf of French bread dipped in olive oil.

They were cracking up at a childhood memory of Steph tattling on Anna for coloring on the walls in the living room when the wail of sirens pierced their bubble of joy.

"Fire trucks," Steph observed as the horns sounded. "More than one, too."

"Wow, I hope it's just a drill and no one is hurt," Cee-cee added around a mouthful of bread.

"Sounds like it's heading toward the beach," Anna said. It wasn't until the words left her lips that her stomach dropped. "You don't think—?" But before she could get the words out, Cee-cee's phone began to buzz on the kitchen island.

Cee-cee reached for it, concern furrowing her brow. "Hello?"

Steph and Anna stared at her in silence, waiting for some sign that it was nothing. Everything was all right.

A second later, her sister's face crumpled and she let out a wail that chilled Anna to the core.

"No, no, no, no!"

"What?" Steph demanded, her face going bone white as she clutched at Cee-cee's shoulder. "What is it?"

Cee-cee shot to her feet and shoved her phone in her purse frantically. "We've got to go right now. That was Mr. Connelly. He's parked across the street from Pop's and said the house is engulfed in flames."

Chapter Twenty-Three

Stephanie was the calmest of the three of them, plus she'd only had half a glass of wine, so she grabbed her keys to drive everyone over to Pop's house.

As Celia got in the front passenger seat, she wondered how her sister could be so collected. What if Pop had been trapped inside? What if he was having one of his spells and couldn't find his way out because of the smoke?

She shook her head. She couldn't let her mind go there. Pop would be fine.

"What else did he say?" Anna asked from the backseat, her voice shaky.

"Uhhh…" she stammered, struggling to form coherent thoughts. "Just what I told you. Pop's house is on fire."

"A room?" Anna asked. "The entire house? And where's Pop? Is he with a neighbor?"

"I don't know, Anna," Celia said in frustration. "I told you everything Mr. Connelly told me. The house is engulfed in flames."

"Don't go borrowing trouble," Stephanie said, her voice even and her eyes on the road. "We need to get there."

"How can you be so calm?" Celia demanded. "Pop might be—" She cut herself off.

"He might be," Stephanie said, "and we hope to God he's fine. But losing our heads isn't going to help anything. We need to get there and get more information. The more collected we are, the better we can help if needed."

"She's right," Anna said, placing a hand on Celia's shoulder. "The only thing we can do is wait."

"And thankfully, I only live a few minutes away," Stephanie added.

Celia knew they were right, but the screaming sirens made her stomach churn. The moment Stephanie pulled up to the curb diagonal to the house—the closest space given the crush of fire trucks and people—Celia had her door open and was jumping out. Her sisters shouted her name, but she ignored them as she raced across the street, pushing her way through the crowd. She could only think of Pop. Her head became fuzzy when she saw the house. Flames shot out of the bottom windows and thick dark smoke rolled out of the top window, darkening the sky above them. The firefighters' hoses were splayed across the front yard as they sprayed high-pressure streams of water at the flames.

She stared at the inferno, her mouth hanging open, completely frozen and overwhelmed.

"Oh, my word," Stephanie gasped behind her, her voice finally cracking just a little.

Anna released a garbled cry. "Pop!"

That shook Celia out of her daze, and her head swiveled as she searched the crowd for a stooped, elderly man with a semi-circle of gray hair around his head. "Pop!" She turned to Stephanie, subconsciously drawn to her relative calm and control. "I don't see him anywhere."

Stephanie took her hands and gave them a little shake. "We'll find him. He got out. I know it."

"But we *don't* know that," Celia countered, her voice breaking. "He could still be inside." She glanced back at her sisters. "How did the fire start?" She knew they didn't have any more information than she did, but her thoughts just seemed to keep tumbling out.

"I don't know," Stephanie said, worry etching her face as her gaze lifted to the house.

"We should have disconnected the gas line to the stove," Anna said, sounding more anxious. "We were bringing him all of his meals, there was no reason to keep it connected."

The doctor had explained to Celia that cooking while home alone was a huge risk factor for the elderly, especially those with early onset dementia, which she'd relayed to her sisters.

"We don't know that it was the stove," Stephanie said in her calm, commanding tone. "And we removed the knobs. There's no way he could have turned on a burner."

Celia hoped she was right, but she supposed it didn't matter. The house was consumed by fire. At this moment, it didn't matter how it had started. That discussion could come later. "I'm not going to just stand here doing nothing," Anna said, before she rushed over to one of the firefighters standing by a fire engine. "Our father lives here! Do you know if he got out?"

The firefighter shook his head. "The neighbors told us an elderly man lives here, but no one has seen him."

"No!" Celia cried out.

"Can you go inside and find him?" Anna pleaded.

The firefighter gave her a sympathetic look. "Ma'am, we'll go inside as soon as we get the fire contained enough to do so."

"By then it will be too late!" Celia protested.

"They'll go in when they can," Stephanie assured her, wrapping an arm around her sister's back.

Celia burst into tears as she moved toward the barrier the firefighters had put up to keep the neighbors at a safe distance from the flames. "Pop!" she called out in a wail, desperately searching the beach and surrounding area for some sign of him through her tears. "Pop!"

Her knees collapsed and Stephanie tried to hold her up, but Celia was too light-headed to remain upright. Stephanie helped her down to the curb and lowered her head between her legs.

"Just take deep breaths, Cee-cee. Deep breaths."

"How can you be so calm?" Anna snapped over Celia's head.

"I'm trained to be calm in a crisis," Stephanie said. "I can't freak out when trauma cases show up in my clinic. So I've learned to handle the situation, then freak out later."

Celia lifted her head to look up at her sisters. "I'm so scared."

"I am, too," Stephanie said with tears in her eyes, "but I refuse to believe the worst. Not yet."

Celia nodded. Her sister was right.

"I'm not going to stand here and do nothing," Anna said firmly. "I'm going to look for him."

"That's a good idea," Stephanie said. "Cee-cee, you should go, too."

"No," she protested. "I need to stay here in case he shows up."

"I'll stay," Stephanie said. "You go with Anna."

The two sisters spent the next ten minutes walking up and down the neighborhood, looking for their father in backyards and front porches—any place he might have gone to escape the sirens and confusion.

No one had seen him.

"We should call Steph and see if she knows anything yet," Anna said with worry in her eyes.

"I didn't bring my phone," Celia said. "Did you?"

"No. I left my purse in Steph's car."

Anxiety knotted in Celia's stomach. "Maybe we should go back so we can call Max and make sure everything was okay when she dropped by to see him earlier." Celia could only imagine the fear and guilt her daughter would feel upon learning that Pop had set the house on fire not long after she'd left him.

Especially if he was inside.

"Good idea," Anna said, and the two sisters hurried back to their father's house.

As they reached Stephanie, a loud groan came from the house and the roof collapsed. Flames shot out of the downstairs windows as the fire gained new life.

All three sisters cried out as the gathering crowd behind them let out gasps and cries of disbelief. Celia wanted to be hopeful, but she knew in her heart there was no way Pop could survive that.

She grabbed her sisters' hands, clinging on for dear life. Although she'd come to terms with the fact that her father's health was deteriorating, she couldn't imagine losing him this way.

The firefighters had begun to get the blaze under control and one of the neighbors suggested the sisters come to her house to wait for word about their father. Celia considered accepting, but she knew she'd crawl out of her skin if she were cooped up inside.

Squeezing Anna and Stephanie's hands, she said, "I want to walk on the beach."

She'd half expected them to call her crazy, but they agreed that watching their family home burn like a funeral pyre wasn't helping any of them calm down.

They walked down the street, past several houses, then took the path down to the beach. She'd taken this path more times than she could count while they were growing up, but she rarely took it now, with the exception of the night of their mother's funeral, when all three sisters had walked the beach together. The fact they were doing the same thing now wasn't lost on her.

Without uttering a word, they turned south, heading down the shoreline behind their father's house, their feet sinking into the soft sand. The air reeked of smoke and dark gray plumes filled the air above the ruins of the house.

Celia noticed the beach was fairly empty of people—they were likely all gawking at the fire. But about a hundred yards ahead, she saw a lone figure walking toward them. Something about his gait seemed familiar.

Stephanie gasped. "Oh my word. Is that...?"

All three sisters took off running toward the stooped silhouette in the distance. When they got closer, they noticed his soot-covered face and clothes.

"Pop!" Celia cried out in relief, then nearly fell over when she saw who was trailing him.

"Who's that with him?" Anna asked, but her tone made it clear she knew.

"I can't believe it," Celia said. Trailing her father was none other than her ex-husband.

"Look who I found," Nate called to them with a shaky smile.

Chapter Twenty-Four

P op!" Celia shouted as she rushed through the sand to throw her arms around him. Anna and Steph joined in a moment later. Her father smelled of smoke, oily and acrid, and he was covered in ash, but she'd never been so happy to ruin a set of clothes in her life. "Pop, are you okay?" she demanded, pulling back to stare into his confused but very much alive face.

"I was on my way out and saw him wandering down the beach," Nate said, raking a shaky hand through his hair. "I called to him, but he didn't hear me over the sound of the sirens. That's when I put it all together. I tried to get him to let me drive him, but he wouldn't have it. He said he was looking for Mittens and he wasn't going back until he found her. So we were taking our time walking back, looking for the cat along the way." He turned his attention to her father and rubbed his shoulder gently. "He's coughing a bit on and off, but other than that, he seems right as rain. Right, Pop?"

Pop let out a string of wheezy coughs in reply, but when he caught his breath, he turned toward Nate and scowled. "Don't call me that. You left my baby girl, I'm not your Pop anymore."

Anna let out a bark of laughter. "Guess he remembers some stuff."

To Nate's credit, he nodded and shot Celia a wry smile. "I'd expect nothing less. I deserved that."

Stephanie swiped at the tears on her face with trembling hands and sucked in a breath. "Okay. Everything is all right. Let's get him the rest of the way home where the emergency personnel are so he can get checked out," she said, back in control, where she felt most comfortable. "Smoke inhalation kills more people than flames do and older people are much more susceptible."

The five of them—Nate included—made their way down the beach with a disoriented Pop making half-hearted calls for Mittens. By the time they got to what was left of the house, half the town was there, heads bowed as the firemen fought the still-burning blaze. Twenty yards away, she could see Max and Gabe huddled together, a little away from the crowd.

"Hey!" she called out, rushing ahead of their little group. "We've got him! He's okay!"

A few people turned to face them and a murmur passed through the crowd.

"It's Red!"

"Red made it!"

"He's alive!"

Max and Gabe both wheeled around to face them and Max's face instantly crumpled into sobs.

"Mom! Dad! Oh, thank God Pop's okay!"

She ran toward them with Gabe following close behind, and launched herself at her grandfather. "Pop, you did so good! You knew there was a fire and you got out! I'm so glad you're all right," she murmured, peppering his dirty face with kisses.

"Ah, cut it out, will ya. I'm only alive for a little while longer. Your grandmother's going to give me hell for cooking that bacon on high heat."

The sisters all shared a look.

Unless that was his imagination, too, Pop must have found a way to turn on the stove despite them removing the control knobs.

The cold, stark reality of the situation hit Celia in the gut. Their current situation was no longer working. Pop needed constant care and putting it off had almost cost them all a price far too great to pay.

Her thoughts were put on hold as people poured toward them, all cheering for Pop. Eva from the diner, several women from the Senior's Center, and even Nina Peterson. A paramedic cut through the crowd and assured everyone that Pop would be back shortly before whisking him away for an exam on the back of the ambulance. Anna followed, but Steph stayed behind with Cee-cee.

"I think we're all on the same page," Steph said with a shuddering sigh. "We dodged a bullet today. We've got a lot of decisions to make, but not tonight. Unless they want to keep him at the hospital overnight for observation, he'll come stay with me until we can get our ducks in a row."

Celia nodded, relieved to have that settled, at least. Having him in her apartment would've been a logistical nightmare, not to mention it wouldn't be safe for him to maneuver the stairs. With the immediate future settled, they'd deal with the rest in the coming weeks.

"I'm going to go over and talk to the EMTs and make sure he's all right."

Celia nodded, wrapping her arms around her middle as a gust of wind kicked up. The smell of smoke was almost unbearable now that the dump of adrenaline had begun to drain away, and she covered her mouth with her shirtsleeve.

She looked up to find Max pulling away from her father's embrace and trudging toward the house where Gabe stood, staring mutely at the wreckage.

"They're just saying their goodbyes," Nate murmured, moving closer to Celia.

She couldn't help but note his perfectly tailored tux was ruined. She also couldn't help but note that he didn't seem to care.

Maybe she wasn't the only one who had changed some.

"Look, Nate. I know we haven't exactly been friendly these past months, but I want you to know I really appreciate what you—"

His pocket began to ring and vibrate and he let out a groan.

"I'm so sorry, I'll just be one second. She keeps calling, and if I don't answer, it will never end."

He picked up and spoke into the receiver. "Hey, you go ahead without me. I'm not going to make it." There was a long pause as Celia tried not to listen. "I know, and I'm sorry, but there's been an emergency with Celia's Dad and I need to be here right now." Another pause, during which what could only be described as shrill screeches emitted from the phone, loud enough that Nate wound up pulling it away from his ear and wincing. When they finally ceased, he cradled it to his face. "Mandy, the second I'm done, I'll go home and change and I'll meet you there."

With that, he disconnected and turned his attention back to Celia.

"She doesn't get it, but she will." He looked away, staring off into the ocean for a long moment before returning his gaze to Celia. "I messed up really bad. You didn't deserve that, and I'm sorry. But I will always be here for my kids, and you, and even your cantankerous old man and your crazy sisters if you need me."

His words, combined with his actions tonight, slipped into the locked cage of her heart like a key, releasing the last of her resentment into the night sky to drift away with the smoke.

"I won't, Nate," she said with a gentle smile. "I'm doing really good, but the kids surely will, and I'm so glad to know that they're still a priority. Even though they're grown, they need us sometimes."

"You got that right." They both turned toward the smoldering remains of her father's bungalow and Nate winced. "I knew it was bad when I saw him, but this..."

They were silent, clearly contemplating how much worse things could've been, when a thought hit her and sent a bubble of laughter exploding from her lips. "So you mean to tell me you were going to let him get in your Porsche like *that?*" The horrified expression on his face only made her laugh harder.

He chuckled and turned to face the house, looking self-conscious. "Believe me, even as I offered, my stomach clenched. But I wanted to get him back here as quickly as possible. I tried your cell and you were obviously too busy to check it, so yeah, I was willing to put the old Porsche on the line." He glanced back and gave her a cheesy grin that reminded her of the Nate she'd met long ago. "Do I get a medal? Or at least a hug?"

She shook her head, suddenly exhausted as the weight of the day crashed down on her. "No dice on the medal, a hug is doable."

He curled his arms around her and she returned his embrace. It was comfortable, easy, like a well-worn shoe, but there was nothing more to it than that. No anger, no resentment, no attraction, no urge to take it further. Just two human beings treating each other with kindness and respect. Nate wasn't a monster. He was a flawed person, as they all were. She'd always be loosely tied to him through their children, but she didn't have to please him anymore. And she was good with that.

She pulled back and shot him a smile. "Thanks again, but I've got to make some calls. I left poor Pete to close up the shop alone and didn't get a chance to call and see how it went. I've also got to contact..." She trailed off as she saw a familiar figure moving away from her, toward a line of cars down the street. A little thrill shot through her and she patted Nate on the filthy lapel. "Why don't you say goodbye to the kids and head over to Mandy's function? I think we've got it all under control now."

He nodded and gave her a wave before heading over to Max and Gabe, but she didn't stand by to watch their interaction.

She sprinted toward the retreating silhouette in the distance. When she was a few yards away, she called out. "Mick!"

Mick turned and lifted his hand in greeting. "I don't want to intrude. I was at the diner and heard the sirens, then someone said it was Red's house. I tried to call first...anyway, you can go ahead back. We can talk later now that I know everyone is okay."

His words sounded one way, but his face was saying something entirely different.

"Is everything okay with *you*?" she asked, closing the distance between them and lacing her fingers with his. "You look miserable."

"Yes." He grimaced and shook his head. "Actually, no. Look, I understand that sometimes moments like this make things seem clearer. If you and Nate are getting back together, I'll respect that." He squeezed her hand and then let it go with a low growl. "I won't understand it, but I'll respect it. At the same time, I can't stand by and be your friend and watch you with him. Not anymore. Not when I know you deserve better."

Celia's mind was reeling as she stared into Mick's lean, handsome face. Did he honestly think she could ever...would ever take Nate back?

"You're right, Mick. I do deserve better."

She leaned up and gripped his broad shoulders, tugging him toward her until he was low enough to kiss.

"And the fire did make things clear for me. Nate leaving was the best thing that ever happened to me. I'm on an amazing new path and I can't wait to create the next chapters of my life. My hope is that you'll be by my side helping me write them."

A relieved grin lit up his face as he drew her into his embrace. "Just try and stop me."

Chapter Twenty-Five

Cee-cee's Cupcakes was bustling. Between the afternoon cupcake-decorating workshops for the kids and the new three-week baking class for adults that Celia had recently initiated, she was getting publicity from several local newspapers. She'd even done a local television interview. After that, several travel websites had covered her shop, making her a popular tourist destination in Bluebird Bay. She and Nina Peterson were discussing adding a cookie-decorating class in the mornings next season since Nina's shop was too small to host her own.

Max's bookstore was still struggling, just as Celia had feared, but Max insisted she had no regrets. Life was simpler in Bluebird Bay. Sure, she was still working long hours, but at least she was working for herself. Nevertheless, Celia was worried about her baby girl. Although she'd vowed to stop taking on other peoples' problems, she'd left a little pile of Max's business cards on the display case at the shop and made sure to mention it whenever tourists asked about things to do in the area.

Gabe and Sasha were not only back together, but engaged again and planning the wedding for sometime next year. The counseling had helped them both. Gabe had finally realized the breakup wasn't about a missed appointment. Although he'd seen his long hours as an investment in their lives together, Sasha had wanted him around more. Surprisingly, Nate was the one who'd given him a talking-to about finding a better work-life balance, a lesson he wished he'd learned himself when the kids were small.

Pop had started working for Celia every afternoon since the fire two weeks ago, which gave him the interaction with people he so desperately craved and also made him feel useful. There was no doubt that his quirky personality had become a draw, especially when he occasionally stood outside the shop and offered samples to passersby. He stood out there today, greeting tourists with samples of a couple of Celia's newest features—Mango Madness and Devil's Red Velvet. A few reviews had mentioned him and, the day before, someone had come in specifically looking for him. The tourist had taken a selfie with Pop then posted on social media, tagging the shop. The post had gotten several thousand likes, and Max had requested that Pop start working part-time in her bookstore, too.

For now, Pop was living with Stephanie, and Celia couldn't determine if it was going well or not. While her sister seemed to have more patience with Pop—she was sure the caregivers they'd hired helped ease the strain—Celia could tell that something was eating at her sister. She wasn't sure if it was the added pressure of dealing with Pop while his place was being rebuilt, or if she was still preoccupied about the strange note she'd found in Paul's things. Whatever it was, Steph wasn't talking and had insisted everything was fine.

The bell on the shop dinged, and Anna walked in, her hair wild and her cheeks rosy, a tell-tale sign she'd been walking the beach. It was her little sister's last day in town before her next photography assignment.

Celia walked around the counter to give her a bear hug. "You still leaving this afternoon?"

"Yep," Anna said, but her smile didn't quite reach her eyes.

"Try to do a better job of keeping in touch," Celia said, rubbing her arm. "I worry about you on those dangerous assignments."

"I'll be fine. I promise I'll do my best to keep in contact, but some of the locations I'll be at don't have internet or cell service."

"Then maybe let me know ahead of time before you go out to those locations, okay?"

Anna's smile was genuine. "Okay."

"I'll miss you." Celia nodded toward their father. "And so will Pop."

"I'm gonna miss you all, too." And for the first time, Celia wondered if Anna didn't want to go anymore.

Just as Celia was about to ask, Anna gave her another hug. "I've gotta go. I just wanted to say goodbye to you and Pop one last time. I'll drop by and see Stephanie, too."

That was different. Anna usually came and went as she pleased. Sometimes Celia didn't even know she was back until she'd had a few days to decompress in her apartment. She'd certainly never made a point of telling them goodbye the day that she left.

"Is everything okay, Anna?"

"Right as rain." Her mouth tugged into a smile. "Behave yourself while I'm gone. Don't do anything I wouldn't do."

Celia laughed. "Is there anything you *wouldn't* do?"

Anna took a step backward, pointing her finger at her with a wink. "Good point."

Two families walked through the door and Celia hurried back to her post behind the counter, but she kept an eye on her sister as she gave their father a long hug and a kiss on the cheek, then rushed out the door with more urgency than necessary.

Celia was even more worried than she'd been before, but the afternoon rush came, and before she knew it, Eva Hildebrand walked in the door, calling out, "Come on, Red! Let's blow this joint!"

"Can't you see I'm busy, woman?" he retorted, holding out his tray.

Eva propped a hand on her hip and gave him a sly look. "I've got meatloaf from Mo's in the car and it's not gonna eat itself."

"Well why didn't you say so?" Pop set his tray on an empty table. "Cee-cee, I'm out of here!"

She laughed as he quickly untied his apron and tossed it over the back of a chair.

Hiring Eva to help watch Pop a few days a week had been Anna's best idea ever. Eva was a God-send who had turned a despondent Pop into the lively version who was currently leaving the shop. Confronted with the indisputable truth that he'd caused the fire—he'd found a pair of pliers to turn on the burner, sly old devil—he'd agreed he couldn't be alone anymore, but it hadn't been easy for him. His verbal sparring sessions with Eva had helped. So had his role at the cupcake shop. But Celia knew this was only a temporary solution. Pop wouldn't hear of selling the lot, so they were in the process of getting bids to rebuild his house. Everyone knew him moving back home would only work if he had someone living with him full time, but Celia couldn't help worrying that he'd end up in an assisted living center anyway. There was no denying his forgetful spells and dementia were becoming more frequent, but that was a worry for another day.

She sent Pete home at five and was about to head downstairs to prep for tomorrow's cupcakes when she heard the front door ding.

"I'm sorry. We're closed," she said as she spun around to greet her customer, but a smile spread across her face when she saw Mick standing in the doorway.

"Then I timed this perfectly," Mick said with an ornery grin, one hand shoved in his front jeans pocket.

Her stomach did a loopty-loop, a now familiar feeling when she saw him. She was sure this feeling should have faded by now, yet it only seemed to grow stronger. "Hey, you."

Walking in, he reached behind him and locked the front door. "Hey, yourself."

"I thought you were working late. I was about to start a batch of cupcakes for tomorrow."

"Then I'll help you," he said, closing the distance between them.

She laughed. "I bet you never saw yourself becoming a baker after the age of fifty."

"I never saw myself doing a lot of things I'm currently doing." He wrapped his arm around her back and tugged her closer, planting a sweet kiss on her lips. "I'm not complaining."

"Me neither," she said with a laugh.

She wouldn't have it any other way.

About the Author

Denise Grover Swank was born in Kansas City, Missouri and lived in the area until she was nineteen. Then she became nomadic, living in five cities, four states and ten houses over the course of ten years before she moved back to her roots. She speaks English and smattering of Spanish and Chinese which she learned through an intensive Nick Jr. immersion period. Her hobbies include witty Facebook comments (in own her mind) and dancing in her kitchen with her children. (Quite badly if you believe her offspring.) Hidden talents include the gift of justification and the ability to drink massive amounts of caffeine and still fall asleep within two minutes. Her lack of the sense of smell allows her to perform many unspeakable tasks. She has six children and hasn't lost her sanity. Or so she leads you to believe.

For more info go to: dgswank.com or denisegroverswank.com

About the Author

Christine Gael is the women's fiction writing alter-ego of USA Today Bestselling contemporary romance author, Christine Bell, and NYT Bestselling paranormal romance author, Chloe Cole.

Christine lives with her sweet, funny husband in South Florida, where she spends the majority of her day writing and consuming mass amounts of coffee. Her favorite pastimes include playing pickle ball and tennis year-round, and texting pictures of palm trees and the beach to her New England-based friends in the wintertime.

While Christine enjoys all types of writing but, at age 46, she's especially excited to be creating stories that will hopefully both entertain and empower the women in her own age group.

For more information visit her website at christinegael.com